The Truth Now

The Truth Now

Anthony Caplan

Thanks to the carers: all the social workers, counselors, teachers, parents, activists, and friends who struggle with containing the epidemic of loneliness.

"Whate'er betide, one human soul
Is knit with mine."
Edward Elgar

Wo aber Gefahr ist, wächst
Das Rettende auch.
Friedrich Holderlin

I - The Last of the Beothuk

As a football player at Ferncroft Regional High School, Sid had been capable of impressive feats, such was the strength of his massive thighs and upper body, not any spring in his naturally archless and large feet, splayed to the side always as he walked. He was out on State Street, free for the first time in 19 years. The sun was shining, casting the world in the anonymous, metallic color of cars. They flowed in both directions, as the wind blew in low black clouds from the northwest, the direction of the correctional facility and the mouth of Sid's past. Sid walked south, shuffling in the prison issue, black pleather boots a couple of sizes too big. His feet throbbed with a dull pain. He had flat feet; the ROTC program had turned him down for it the spring before his freshman year at the University of New Hampshire. Wearing the prison issued boots that denied him access to the rec yard, Sid had consistently gained weight and lost count of the days, of the hours, and of friends and family. It had all flowed unconditionally, a numbed-out, accumulating rush, until he'd dreamed of his release as a void. He'd long ago forgotten exactly what he'd done. In fact he claimed not to ever have had any recollection. His innocence was like the boots: ungainly, impractical, synthetic, and had never come off in all the seasons of the years, despite the stares of the parole board like maddened owls.

Following some interior reckoning system that led him uphill, Sid walked away from the thicker traffic flows. He saw a wrought iron fence ahead in the distance. In the park, there were children playing on some recently constructed playground equipment, sliding into a sandpit that was wet and puddled from the last rain, with a skim of some sort on the water. Sid found a bench with a small round stone someone had left on the end of it. He sat on the bench and watched, playing with the stone in his fingers. It was weathered and smooth to the touch. A dog came up and sniffed at his boots. Sid let it be, not wanting to impact the waves of feeling flowing through him for the first time, as his senses awakened and his head throbbed. The dog was a young pup of indeterminate breed, with intelligent looking eyes as it studied him. Sid let the thoughts form in his head that drew the dog close. He dropped his hand with the stone in it, and the dog sniffed, drawing conclusions. A small boy appeared out of a slide and ran across the grass to the bench.

"Hey, Boy! Come 'ere," said the boy, kneeling and waving his hands.

"Is he your dog?" asked Sid. At least that's what he thought he'd said.

The boy kept his head down. Maybe the sound had emanated from underground. Or perhaps he couldn't hear. Sid realized he needed to speak louder through the thick growth of his beard.

"IS HE YOUR DOG?"

"I guess so," said the boy.

"How much you want for him?"

"I don't know."

"I'll give you twenty bucks for him."

The boy stared. Sid drew out five twenty dollar bills from the front pocket of his prison issue slacks, stretching his legs. The dog jumped back and looked around on his haunches.

"He ain't really mine." The boy was standing there, scratching his head.

"Well, whose is he then?" asked Sid.

"I don't know. He's just always around. He's been here as long as I can remember."

"Well, that's not very long. He's just a pup. Here." Sid stood and handed over a bill from the roll, his massive frame looming over the boy. The boy took the bill from Sid's hand and stared as if at an unfamiliar object, not sure of its use or legitimacy.

"It's real," said Sid. "It's my gate money. I guess that makes it official. Everything has to have a price to make it real. What'd you say his name was?"

But the boy had run off, scared by all the words Sid had thrown his way.

The dog didn't have a name. Sid thought that in time perhaps one would come to him. There were a lot of things out there that had no name. Most things in fact, were unnamed. Of all the things in the universe, the larger percentage by far were like the dog, who existed without having a known name. Somebody might have given him a name. Besides having a known price, that's all it took to bring him into the real world of people, cars, streets, and parks like this one he sat in now.

When Sid dropped his hand, the dog came sniffing for food. The lack of food was a problem that did have a name, and its solution, like everything, would come in due time. Sid was feeling equanimous in his new free state, despite his lack of connections to anybody but a dog.

He stayed on the park bench. The dog came and went. It knew its way around. Groups of children played in the distance around a pond, throwing bread crumbs at the geese that overwintered there or perhaps were early arrivals. The dog tried to get their attention, sniffing the bread crumbs in the air as they flew from the children's hands. The wind was an acquaintance that had changed over the years but could be recognized by the way it moved and pinched his ears. Sid shuffled on the bench and drew his coat tighter around his middle with his massive, numbed hands. The dog appeared, sniffing the wind as if it could sense a contagion. Sid picked it up and stuck it next to him on the bench. He felt that the dog was a creature that had appeared as if out of a dream, an augury of some sort of the final days. It curled up and went to sleep there on the bench. The sun went down. The night, interminable and silent, gave up none of its secrets. Sid woke in the morning from the pain of his frozen buttocks hanging over the edge of the park bench.

He stood and stiffly went off in search of food. The dog was gone. Exiting the park, Sid walked down a side street of nice, new houses. The gas station on the corner looked like it might have some food. Two small men speaking in a language Sid did not understand stopped talking as Sid moved around the inside of the mostly empty place, stomping his boots loudly to lose the pain in his feet. The store looked like it had recently been the scene of some change in ownership, with unstocked shelves and darkened walls of bare chipboard next to the smoky plate glass looking out at the two pumps. There was one aisle that was not completely bare. For some reason it contained items: paper plates, bags of cat litter, puppy food, boxes of green foiled Chocolate Chip Pop Tarts, and orange boxes of vacuum-wrapped Mega Snack Lunchables. Sid felt blessed to have come across this oasis of exactly what he needed. He felt again liberated and back in the world of America that he'd last inhabited in a haze in 1997. Bill Clinton had been president. The whining voice of the radio man, Rush Limbaugh, had castigated and exhorted. The winter sky in his hometown had slowly tumbled into a spring green with envy.

The two men resumed their conversation. Sid took his items, four Lunchables, four Pop Tarts, a small bag of Purina Puppy Chow, and went in search of a cash register. One of the men moved off in the direction of the far wall, and Sid followed, his hands splayed out in front of him filled with the goods and the bag of puppy food clutched under his arm.

The man rang up the items. He finally looked up and studied Sid's eyes.

"You have a dog," said the man.

"Yeah," said Sid. "I'll have a coffee, too."

"Regular?"

"Yeah. Lots of sugar."

"Sugar's bad for you," said the man, his sing-song, exotic accent making it sound somehow more malign, as if lumped in with lots of the nameless and missing items on the dark shelves.

"Lots of things are bad for you," said Sid.

He took his puppy chow and the plastic bag full of food in one hand and the coffee in the other and walked back to the park. He drank the coffee and crumpled the styrofoam cup. Now he was feeling better, and he sat back on the bench where he'd spent the night and waited for the dog to appear. Sid fell asleep and dreamed for a while and woke up, feeling disoriented, oddly out of sorts. It would take getting used to being free, he guessed. He wished he had some drugs to take the edge off reality. It seemed oppressively much larger than he was used to.

A woman pushing a young girl in a stroller approached on the walking path. Sid studied the woman and the child. Her face pushed Sid back into his memories. She looked like Yolanda, his stepmother, the woman who had cared for Sid and his brother after their mother had left. His father, Steve Green-Smith, had been an artist and never concerned much with the details of child-rearing. For a few years Sid and Darrell had run amok, but then Yolanda had managed to calm things down with the town police and the school. Sid had played football with a violent abandon that sprung from some mysterious source, and soon he was being approached and cultivated by the defensive staff at UNH, so that meant special treatment from most of the town elders.

Yolanda had wanted things to be better, with a steadfast belief that one day they would be. She believed in Steve's talent and tried always to keep him busy producing the turned wooden work and the abstract ceramic pieces, like the pack of wolves he'd sold to the Kearsarge Indian Museum. Without Yolanda, Steve would have sunk, Sid surmised. Steve liked to claim with grandiosity, in moments of vulnerability perhaps, that he was the last of the Beothuk, the People of the Dawn.

The woman stopped and checked on the young girl in the stroller.

"Do you want some juice, Leesha?"

"Yes," said the little girl. She must have been five or six, Sid guessed. The woman was probably in her mid-forties.

"Nice day," he ventured.

"Yes, it is," said the woman, looking briefly up at him as she unscrewed the top on a Gatorade bottle and handed the bottle to the girl.

"Why doesn't she walk? She could use the exercise," said Sid.

"That's true," said the woman. This time she didn't look back at Sid, but stayed attentively waiting for the little girl to finish drinking from the bottle.

"Good for kids to walk."

"Good for everyone," said the woman.

"I could walk forever," said Sid.

"You better get started. Forever goes quick," said the woman.

"That's funny," said Sid.

"What's your name?" asked the woman.

"Sid Green. You look like someone. What's your name?"

"Ruth."

"Ruth what?"

"Rendell."

"What kind of name is that?"

"I don't know."

"You look like my stepmother."

"Oh," said Ruth.

"Yeah, she was a good woman," Sid lied.

Ruth shifted her weight and leaned on the handles of the stroller.

"You have some free time?" she asked.

"Yeah," said Sid.

"I could use a favor." She coughed.

"Well, I think I should let you know, I can't go anywhere without my dog," said Sid, stroking his beard.

"Where is he?" asked Ruth, looking intently at him. He was a person of interest now that he had a dog. Sid smiled inside, thinking of the irony.

"There he is," said Sid, glancing the dog out of the corner of his eye. It was like the dog was suddenly interested in Sid also. It was funny how he was leveraging himself back into the complications of daily living. Sid squinted into the distance as the dog approached. He didn't trust any of it.

"There you go, boy. I got you some food," said Sid, ripping open the bag of puppy chow on the bench next to him. He scooped inside with his hand and brought out a handful of dried tidbits. Some spilled on the ground, and the dog leaped on the morsels with great speed.

"Wow. For a puppy he's really hungry," said Ruth.

"Yeah, he is," said Sid.

"He's a boy. Isn't he? What's his name?"

"I don't know. I haven't thought of it yet. I'm not sure if he's a he. Could be a she."

"Okay. I'll get to the point." She laughed a scratchy laugh as if she had a throat infection, some nasal drip. "You help me move a treadmill, and I'll get you some food. How's that? You hungry?"

Sid thought for a second. These were more swamps of a new country that threatened his fragile mental balance. He swallowed hard and chose.

"Yes. I'm not going to lie. I'm starved. Had some Pop Tarts for breakfast, but that was a while ago. I was thinking of heading downtown in a few and finding a restaurant that might have some leftovers or something."

"That's a great idea. But first help me out with the treadmill, huh?"

Ruth explained her situation, attempting to sweeten the deal with personal revelations. Jaydee, an older gentleman, had decided recently to move to Arizona. Jaydee had somehow gotten his hands on a van he'd been converting with the idea that they could all drive out there together, but there had been a problem with the frame. It was incorrigibly rotted at several points, so he'd gone on his own on Southwest without her and Leesha. The van's location was unknown, but it had probably been scrapped. Jaydee was trying to get fit, trying to get clean. He thought they all could use a new start in Arizona. They probably could. The nub of her request was that Jaydee had left a treadmill in the kitchen of her apartment. Ruth was trying to sell it but needed help moving it down the stairs in the entrance.

"You think he's meaning to come back?" asked Sid.

"Does that really matter?"

"I know you're trying to forget him, but it helps to know what he intended. I mean it's technically still his."

"Who's it help?" she asked.

"What?"

"Who's it help, that sort of thinking?"

"It's not who. Just in general it's better to do things right, don't you think?"

"Right? What's that? You think you know what right is? You need food, I need to move the damn treadmill. That's what's right. There ain't no more than that, big guy. Is there?"

"Listen, I don't want to sit and argue with you. I'd like to help. As soon as we figure out what Jaydee meant to do."

"But I need help now. I'm not kidding about that. Screw Jaydee. He ain't coming back. He'd sell his mother if she wasn't nailed down."

There was something in her eyes that Sid hadn't seen in a long time, a sort of fierceness that appealed to Sid's memories.

"I said I'd help."

"You did? When?"

"Just now."

"You can wait for your dog."

"No, let's go. Now. " Sid stood, pitching a little to one side. The woman and the child seemed to size him up, both of them a little startled at how far up he'd stood with the sudden change of mind.

"But what about the dog?" insisted Ruth.

"He'll figure it out," said Sid, not wanting to think about the dog anymore. The dog was an opportunist, like all creatures, and not worth a second thought. If he thought about the dog anymore he would get stuck. That was how his mind worked. But then he saw the dog playing with the geese by the water. He felt remorse, and was reminded again of the difficult choices he would be forced to make every day now. It was almost better in the correctional facility, where he had one overriding objective, to numb himself in any way possible. There were all sorts of ways: walking in circles in the cell, listening to the voices in his head, getting drugs. The most effective and popular sedatives in the correctional facility usually entailed some simple transactions that never involved emotional entanglements. Here now it was different. Here everything was involved all at once. It was paralyzingly complex for a big man, and somehow shameful. He longed for some of those pills again to take him away, even if just for an instant, even for just an edge on the sense of losing.

They left the park up some steps to a gate and through it to the street. They walked uphill, Sid straggling behind Ruth as she pushed Leesha and chatted distractingly to the child. Sid looked back and saw the dog poking out of the gate. He reached into the bag of puppy chow and dropped a couple of pieces on the sidewalk. In this way, he enticed the dog to follow. A name came to him: Rover. It was sort of non-specific, and it fit because it entailed adventure, his as well as the dogs, even though Sid had never been one to stray, really. Only in his mind, and even then in a limited fashion, because he got lost easily. The Beothuk, similarly, had reached the eastern shores of the land. They had stayed for thousands of years always with the sun in the morning water. He felt better walking between the dog and the woman and her child, and when Rover went out ahead of him on the sidewalk, Sid looked out over his domain and was pleased.

They stopped at a small, dark house with stained clapboards and a vintage Toyota around the side, its rusting rims on cement blocks. Ruth got Leesha out of the stroller, and the little girl ran heartily around on the wet, moss-covered paving stones to the spongy back porch. Sid was surprised by her burst of energy. He was breathing heavily.

“This is it,” said Ruth, looking back at him.

Sid stared at her as if he were lost.

"Come in," she said.

Sid walked up to the back door where Ruth waited, holding the screechy screen door open.

"The dog can come in, too," she said, "Come on, dog," she called.

"His name is Rover," said Sid.

"That's a nice name," said Ruth proudly.

The screen door slammed.

Sid felt awkward inside the apartment. Ruth told him where to go, how to stand, when to lift the treadmill. They got it down the stairs to the foyer beside the unused front door. Sid pushed the dog out of the way with his boot. He watched pedestrians in the afternoon through the fogged yellow square of glass in the front door. He was inside.

He had scraped his hand on the bannister. It was bleeding on the shag carpeting. Ruth pushed him over to the kitchen sink. She gave him some paper from a toilet roll next to the sink, and he wiped the blood away where it had pooled on the linoleum of the dark kitchen. He sat at the kitchen island for a long time holding the toilet paper around his hand. Ruth vaped some in the living room, and Leesha fell asleep in a makeshift hammock devised with a scarf and some hooks in the doorway of a utility closet under the stairs.

Ruth came over and offered him a hit.

"Thanks," said Sid, inhaling deeply.

"It'll help with the pain," she said.

She stroked his hand.

"You were a big help," said Ruth. Sid looked her in the eyes. She smiled. They made love, moving to the sofa in the living room. Sid blacked out, and when he came to he had his good hand around her neck on the shag carpet. She was writhing beneath him. He lay there on top of her, trembling. Ruth continued to pleasure herself. At last she trembled wildly. Sid rolled over. He was so excited that he could do it again. After nineteen years, getting off with a woman was a big moment, and he wanted to repeat it as soon as possible. Ruth did what she could. Sid's bad hand throbbed in a dull pain.

Afterwards, she showed him pictures of Notre Dame on her phone. It was burning. The spire had collapsed. She thought it would make him feel better.

"That shit's too bad," said Sid.

"Bad things happen."

"Yeah, they do."

"Do you have a girlfriend, Sid?"

"No."

"D'you just kill 'em?"

"Hey, don't say that."

Sid sat up and found his pants.

"Look, I was just kidding," said Ruth.

He pulled his pants on. Then he rummaged around on the floor until he found his boots under the sofa. He sat on the floor pulling them on with just one hand.

"Where are you going?" asked Ruth. She was peering at him from the sofa, sitting with a blanket over her, arms crossed judgmentally.

"I don't know," answered Sid, sounding pained, suddenly far away.

"You don't have to go. You can stay here, you know."

"I can't stay here," said Sid, anguish apparent in his voice.

"Why not? What is it?"

"What it is is I just spent nineteen years in jail. Nineteen fucking years for a crime I didn't do. Okay? I didn't do it. But I couldn't prove it."

Sid sniffed. His boots were hard to get on. He stood up and tried to stand into them, but the attempt hurt his feet, and he sat on the end of the sofa.

"That's okay." Ruth wanted to comfort him.

But Sid was back on the boat launch behind the church. He had been there many times in his mind in the intervening years. The air coming off the river was cold and wet. The roar of the water blanked out any thoughts, and above the branches of the trees to the west the moon sat in the dawn light, an evil crescent mocking him with its missing piece, as if it was his brain. He was soaking wet and Meg was not there.

The canoe was on its side in the river, pinned against rocks in a sandy spit below.

"That's where she should be," he thought. The thought, the sureness of its recurrence, was the only proof, the article of faith that cemented his blameless soul. She must have fallen out when they overturned, hit her head on a rock in the rapids and washed downstream where the police search and rescue team found her later in the day in the late afternoon sun, on the muddy bank, under a highway bridge. They raced down there in a squad car with the full alarm going. He crashed through the undergrowth ahead of two cops. It was the last time he'd moved so fast, but it was too late. Her bloated body, her swollen face, the flies -- he had never gotten over the burn of it on him. He had tried to explain that to the petrified faces of the parole board.

In nineteen years, what Sid could safely say was that his interior life continued to bear its forked stamp and continued to prove crooked. Despite the strain, the contradiction between what he knew and what they knew, life went on. For nineteen years, it went on like the river, flowing from its mysterious sources and on, into the wild, unknowable galactic ocean, the universal mouth of everything, from where it would one day return and begin again in some mysterious process that was like the moon, like his brain. And now it was no different besides the fact that he, the Sid Green that had taken up space uselessly and at public expense for so long that he had mistaken it for eternity, had now popped free at last like a water-logged stick, like a swamped canoe from the ice-blocked current and swept downstream to a new country, around a bend where the Beothuk could once again breathe in secret, hidden from the genocidal strain that had spread over the skin of the Earth.

Sid went back to the park, but two days later was there in the afternoon to help when the man arrived to pick up the treadmill. He said it was for his wife who was training for a five kilometer race. She had hurt her knee. The orthopedic specialist had recommended starting the rehab with slow runs on a treadmill. The man was driving a Subaru wagon with the back seats down. Sid carried the treadmill over to the car, dragging it swiftly across the paving stones and the bumps in the curb. He hefted one end into the trunk and pushed the rest of it in with his hands. He didn't know what to say to the man when he handed him the check.

"Is everything good?" asked the man, noticing that Sid was studying the check.

"It's fine," said Sid.

"It's crazy that we're still using checks. You know, in Europe they just don't exist. Gone completely over to, like Venmo and what have you," said the man. Sid stared at him.

"It's fine," he repeated. "She'll be happy it's gone."

Ruth was sitting in the kitchen feeding Leesha. Rover looked up and barked when Sid came in the back door. He handed Ruth the check.

"Oh, good. I'm so happy it's out of here at last," said Ruth.

"Well, I'll be on my way," said Sid.

"No you don't," said Ruth. "You'll stay for dinner. I'm making your favorite."

"What is that?"

"Mac and cheese."

"How'd you know?"

"And turkey breast. It was on sale at Market Basket."

"How'd you know?"

"You told me, Sid. You don't remember."

"I don't remember shit. My mind is fouled up, Ruth."

"Sit down and have some tea."

"I don't drink tea."

"Play with Leesha."

"I don't play with little girls."

"Jesus Christ. Stop being a douchebag."

"I'll play with Rover. He remember me?"

"He does. He goes back to the park to find you every morning."

Sid stayed that night, and that next morning tried to explain to Ruth what he felt. It came down to the fact that he was drawn to the past more than the future. He tried to explain that the arrow of time was drawing in the opposite direction in his own mind, and the repercussions would make it difficult for anyone who tried to bring him into a life of any ordinary sort.

"Why is that?" Ruth asked, sipping patiently at a mug of tea. She didn't have to be at work until ten that morning. She worked at the Pacha Mama, the boutique on Main Street that sold green home products and also did custom framing.

"I don't know. I guess I'm just looking for answers. Somebody else calling out with the answers like some crazy-assed Bingo game."

"Could you meet me downtown with Leesha?"

"I don't know."

"I can get you some answers."

Sid wondered why Ruth didn't have a television hooked up. She spent a lot of money on Internet service. It seemed like she wasn't doing the best she could to live the dream. She was constantly afraid of the rent going up, of losing hours at Pacha Mama. Afraid that Leesha was sick. Sid wondered what he could do to make her less afraid, but there were a lot of things he didn't know. He didn't trust his own brain.

He found a stack of magazines in the utility closet and was going through them with some interest. They probably belonged to some earlier tenant, even perhaps to the landlord. Ruth described him as a retired optometrist who lived in Franklin and flipped houses on the side with the help of his wife. He read about the Kardashian sisters. He read about the friendship between Obama and Biden. It was like in jail when he'd eavesdropped on conversations between some of the inmates about the Red Sox or about protein supplements. It was all helpful coloration that he could use, maybe later in life, in some new incarnation. You had to swim in the current.

Leesha only slept for half an hour. After that Sid took her for a walk to the park and back. Sid pushed her in the stroller and left Rover off the leash. He only got into trouble once when Rover chased a jogger for a few hundred feet before getting distracted by some piles of leaves. Leesha was content as long as she had a bottle of apple juice or some snackable on the tray in front of her. Sid wondered how long he could hold out in this routine. He tried to relax, sitting on the bench where he'd apparently stopped spending nights, breathing deeply, not thinking about the pile of wasted opportunities rotting in his wake. He knew that with enough time and space, his mind would reverse course and begin casting back, flitting from branch to branch of some tree that connected to the root, the source of his unhappy disease. Everything else was a distraction and would eventually be jettisoned. He was just too strong and too wild. He sat like a rock, immobilized by his self-aware imagination. The world stilled around him, as if he were imperceptibly bending force fields.

It is raining. It must be a metal roof, because the pinging of the rain is deafening. Also, the constant background buzz of a busy bar, bottles clinking, hysterical mid-range laughing, basso profundo shouting of a scrum ranged along the counter. You are seated somewhere in the depths, not too far from the bar. You are aware that it is busy. The crowd mostly taking refuge from the rain. It is early nighttime, hot and humid. The water is gurgling off the roof and pretty rapidly sinking through the asphalt and concrete to subterranean sinkholes and passing to bedrock. The voices echo the rain, words gurgling through ear holes and worming their way through the inner ear and timpani to the grey sponge of minds. Your companion leans in conspiratorially. The night is full of secrets, as if the rain laid bare a network of tendrils.

She had stones. That's how she kept us from getting thirsty. We went day and night. Started out when the sun was starting to go down. She gave us a stone. Put it in our hands and closed our fingers around them. Her hand was always wet after driving because she was nervous. We went through the checkpoints, and she was always nervous. She had a permit because she was a botanist. She had a degree from the University of Freiburg in botanical science. But they didn't allow her to test her theories. Why? Because she was a woman. Grandfather had been shot by the Russians trying to escape from one of the labor camps after the war. They were always suspicious of her allegiance. She had no cause. You were her justification.

She said that plants could communicate with each other. That was her thing, the one thing that she knew was true and nobody else would believe it. We'd go for hours at night with the stone in our mouth, silent, trying to breathe easy. The trees were thin young pines on the sides of hills. Stars poking in between the tops. We'd get to the top, a ridge at tree line where you could see the field of stars opening up at eye level, growing. Like that feeling when you're about to faint, but the opposite.Consciousness growing in you like a tree, as the field of stars expands. And she would suddenly stop and say 'Hor zu, kinder.' Just the two of us, You and me. You could hear things. It was true. I don't know if we all heard the same things. Though it is possible.

In the morning when you returned, the old man was asleep. You were always wet with nerves and exhaustion. The nerves from her. You felt everything she did. Not sure we all heard the same things at the mountain tops, but we felt the same things, the nervous exhaustion because what she was planning was impossible, what she believed was impossible, and she couldn't share it with anybody, not even us. She would only allow you to take the stone out when you were back inside the apartment and you could hear the snores of your father.

The soldiers stationed in Krumlov got used to seeing us every night. They started calling us the night scientists when they stopped us in the old station wagon, the Volga M-22 that she had because she was a professor, not full tenure but on the faculty at the University of West Bohemia, pretty respected for her lab work. She kept her theories about plant communication to herself. They would look inside and shine their flashlights on you asleep in the back seat.

'The night scientist is sleeping well tonight. Research going okay?'

'About right,' she would say, her hands clenching the steering wheel as if the car might get away from her, which was quite possible given the vagaries of the car's manual transmission.

Then they would wave her through, and it was another night at home in the apartment, cleaning up after father, hiding the bottles in the closet under the spare sheets, hiding the bruises under makeup, hiding her secret behind your stone, your expressionless face in school when the teacher prodded you with his finger in the side as he walked down the rows.

'Wake up, Pietrowicz. This is not the country club. The Jews aren't coming to clean up after you and manicure the greens,' he would say. He was a real bastard, that teacher. Some said he was a survivor of Stalingrad. He taught rhetoric and Latin to middle school boys. You remember 'Gallia est omnis divisa in partes tres.'

One night she had you put the cat in a plastic carrying case and packed one light bag with a change of clothes for you and a few dresses. On top of everything she packed a paper shopping bag with some apples, a roll of bread and some hard cheese.

'Hast du die katz?'

'Ya, Mutti.'

And you produced the carrying case with Karl mewing inside half contentedly because he liked you.

We drove and drove what seemed hours on those one lane roads twisting through fields and forest and villages at sunset to Pohorska Vez. We parked in a dirt lot next to an old house, a once formidable estate. She said it had been the summer home of a famous violinist. I can't remember his name. It was a ruin, gate half off its hinges, swallows flitting in and out of the windows. There was a sign next to the road designating the forest a public good, a resource for recreation.

You asked: 'Are we going into the house, Mutti?'

'No, Henry. We are going to Austria. You will never see your father again,' she said. Checking both ways on the road before hauling out the bag and the carrying case with Karl inside. You took the carrying case. I took the bag because I was older and had

refrained from asking her the silly question about the house even though I had been the first to think of it.

'Hold one moment,' she said. 'I almost forgot.'

She took the stones from her purse and handed one to you, curling your fingers around it silently, looking you in the eye carefully for understanding. Now it was time for quiet. The sun had almost disappeared in a final late summer blaze of fire behind some dead trees. You looked at me.

In that instant, I lowered the bag off my shoulder to the ground. I understood that was the way it was going to be. Just you and her going on without me once again. I began to run. Back down the road, to Pohorska Vez. Slowly at first and then gaining speed, like water coming to a boil, Henry. But no, not you. You went on. Like a fool, Henry. On and on, you still go.

Sid shook his head. He pushed the stroller with Leesha asleep in it along the sidewalk and managed to drag Rover behind, constantly stopping to smell and explore. He looked at the people downtown whom he passed on the sidewalk. Old age crept up on them every day, like a rising tide. Even here, in the middle of an afternoon in the full blow of summer, the Earth was sucking its spiral tentacles from the inside of every cell, carrying out the old task, taking here and giving there in the name of the nameless. Splitting and sifting. Sid pushed through the crowd. The homeless people sitting in a doorway looked up at him. They were trying, everyone was trying to resist.

Sid had to remind himself that he'd just come out of jail after nineteen years. It already seemed that long ago. Leesha and Rover were as alive to him as anything or anybody ever had been. That is to say he wasn't sure they weren't a mirage, a projection thrown up by the void, where everything was always falling apart even when it seemed the most beautiful and alive. The streets were, of course, a falsification and meant nothing. Worse than a dream. Snatches of conversation were carried by the wind.

"It was always a joke. They could have asked."

"Nuts on her. She is so unhappy. When do the people get a say?"

"China has got the edge on us. They have years and years to do whatever."

Leesha stirred. She raised her head off the bar where she had rested. Rover took advantage of a momentary halt to run around to the back of a woman and jump up on her calves. She leaned forward, taking the shock.

"I'm sorry. I'm sorry," grumbled Sid, tugging at the leash imperiously. The woman shook her head and half-grinned. She was wearing a business skirt and coat, despite the heat. An office worker, perhaps, in one of the law firms that dotted the downtown. To the east, behind the streets, the Merrimack flowed widely green and sinuous, carving out a path patiently, like a mother, for itself. Sid wondered how to blow the moment up, how to make it apparent that everybody was drugged out on the dream. Everyone's pain was the same. Everyone knew.

There was no blowing it up. You had no choice but to be afraid.

Ruth was there. Outside the shop. Sid saw her first, before she spotted them. He leaned over and looked at Leesha as he pushed. He wondered if she could see that far up the sidewalk. Ruth was with another woman, younger, more subdued in her appearance. Where Ruth was small, wiry, with an intensity, a nervous energy that seemed, even at a distance, to be barely contained, this other woman was large-boned and mild-mannered. Ruth spoke with her hands fluttering animatedly in the air. They had a life of their own. Sid smiled to himself. When he was close enough to come alongside the two, he stopped and straightened, putting his hands in his pockets. With his boot he pressed the lever locking the wheel on the stroller. Without skipping a beat, Ruth bent down and picked Leesha out of the stroller, hoisting her up in her arms.

"Hi there, bootsie. How's Leesha? Yes, you are so right to be angry. How many times have those guys been wrong?"

"Many. But this time…" said the other woman.

"No different. Hi, Sid."

Sid smiled. He leaned down and rubbed Rover behind the ears. "Good boy," said Sid.

"Was it okay today?" asked Ruth, bopping Leesha up and down in her arms and swinging her around. "Wooh!" she went, and Leesha half-smiled.

"I think so. I gave her lunch like you said and she had a nap after we went to the park."

"That's good. Did you have a nap?"

"Nah, I can't sleep in the day. I had a look at the stove. I think I know what's wrong. The front ring needs to be replaced."

"You figured that out?" asked Ruth.

"Yeah."

"Hope that's right. The stove sucks at our house, Lesli," she said.

"Tell the landlord," said Lesli.

"Sid is very good with stuff like that."

Lesli smiled. Ruth stopped swinging Leesha.

"Hi there. You just moved in?" said Lesli.

"Yeah," said Sid. He stood straight again and put his hands back in his pockets.

"He's still getting used to stuff," said Ruth.

"That's good," said Lesli, smiling at Sid. "What's number one on the list, Sid?" she asked.

"I don't know," said Sid. She sounded like a professional carer, one of the growing army of vocationally concerned.

"Getting sleep. Regular sleep pattern," answered Ruth for him.

"Well, that's hard 'cause Leesha always wakes up and wants to come to bed. So…" said Sid.

"Hey," said Ruth, feigning anger.

"Peter doesn't sleep at night either. Never has," said Lesli.

"Really? Where is he now?" asked Ruth.

"He's still around. Heading down to Charlotte anyday. You know," said Lesli.

"You want to do a reading, Sid? She can do a reading for you," said Ruth, turning to Sid.

"What's that?" asked Sid.

"Looking at something you have. If the conditions are good," said Lesli.

"What is it you're looking at?" asked Sid.

"Auras," said Lesli.

"Colors," said Ruth.

"Colors," repeated Sid.

"We all got them, Sid. Energy patterns," said Ruth.

"Sure," said Sid.

Ruth and Lesli looked at each other.

Lesli's car was parked on one of the streets behind the YMCA. Sid got in the back seat with Rover and Leesha, holding Rover in his lap to make room because of all the junk on the floor of the car: books, clothes, kitchenware, soda cans, food wrappers. Lesli had the radio on some pop station that went on when the car started. A voice was selling cars. Lesli turned the radio off. The car synced to her phone, and she called her house. Someone answered, a young man's voice.

"Hello, Lesli? Are you on your way? Is it too late to ask?"

"Yes, Boyd. It's too late. I have people in the car."

"Oh. Well," said the voice.

"I'll see you soon," responded Lesli.

The house was on a long stretch of broken asphalt going into dense woods, a forest of old hemlock with twisted, scattered branches cluttering the undergrowth and bittersweet vines climbing the mossy trunks. It was a low ranch of barn-board siding and had a cinder block chimney at one corner that looked like it might topple. Wind chimes clinked on a small, covered porch. Lesli tried a key, and then the door opened.

"I put the water on and the noodles in," said the boy who had opened the door. He was wide shouldered and short.

"How long ago?" asked Lesli, pushing past him.

"About ten minutes," shouted the boy into the black of the house where she had gone.

"These are my friends, Boyd, let them in," she shouted back.

"Oh," said Boyd, laughing at himself. He stepped out onto the porch, cocked his head and made way as Ruth pushed Leesha by the shoulders.

Rover started to bark and pull on the leash. Sid let him off the leash and followed back down the porch steps as the dog ran off to inspect the areas beyond the edge of the dirt driveway. There were muttering voices as the door closed. Sid looked at the sky between the trees. The Beothuk had been worshipers of the dawn's light. The other tribes of the forest disappeared, but the Beothuk had held out. North was through the trees. Inward, through his heart, was a path littered with debris and dead wood. Rover sniffed at his feet and seemed content to sit on his haunches.

They gathered in the living room, with Sid and Lesli facing each other on the floor surrounded by an assortment of candles set upright and burning in various glasses and bottle caps. On one of the walls hung some guitars and on another draped a lacy sort of fabric. Lesli began by running her hands around Sid without touching. She closed her eyes. Boyd hit the light switch and sat again on a rumpled mattress with Ruth and Leesha. Ruth held Rover and tried to calm him by breathing smoke into his face.

After a long time of running her hands and studying Sid, Lesli sat back on her heels and faced him. Sid was getting sleepy, fighting to retain his concentration.

"There's a light around you, Sid," she said.

"Yeah. What's that mean?"

"Ghosts. Some call them shadows, banshees."

"Yeah. I guess I need an exorcist. You've done what you could," said Sid, smiling.

"Well. The old souls have something to tell you and you need to figure out what it is."

"Can't we just ignore them?"

"What is it they want from you?" asked Lesli.

"They want me to behave myself," said Sid, sitting up onto his elbows after a moment's consideration. "I already know that. I can tell you what they want. They want me to give up fornicating and fighting."

"Yeah. Okay. Do you want me to do a reading? Try to get a sense of who's here with you right now?"

"Sure," said Sid.

"Lie down," commanded Lesli.

The candles flickered as Sid put himself on his back. He closed his eyes. Lying there for a while, he felt silence invade his body like a balm, driving out the disorderly confusion of his jumbled thoughts. He opened his eyes. The light of the candles was like water lapping at him in a shallow.

"No. I can't locate anything right now," said Lesli. Sid sat up and grabbed his knees slowly. Disappointment registered in her eyes. Sid felt sorry for her.

"That's too bad," he said.

"Look, Sid. I want to help you. I'll do anything I can," said Lesli.

"That's very kind of you."

"I mean it. I want you to know I'm here to help if you need me."

"Well, thanks. Maybe it's not so bad." Sid made to stand up. It was over.

"No, it's bad," said Lesli. Sid sat back down on the floor.

"You need to do what you can, otherwise it will destroy you. Write down your dreams. Wake up early every day. Write them down no matter how silly or vague they seem."

After they ate, Boyd and Lesli played music on guitars, sitting on tree stumps they brought in from the hall next to the front door. They set the bowls of food and the remaining loaf of homemade bread aside and brought out some beer Boyd had made.

Boyd sang some John Prine and Miranda Lambert songs. Lesli could do the intro to *Over the Hills and Far Away.*

"*Ta-da-da-da, da-dee-da-da-da... Hey lady,*" sang Sid. Lesli and Ruth smiled.

"No, that's good, Sid," said Boyd.

Sid tried Lesli's idea of waking up early to write down his dreams. The problem he found was that his dreams were slippery. They morphed in the second between Ruth's alarm and when he raised his head with the conscious thought that it was him dreaming and not the dream that contained him in it. Had those been seals or was it a flock of birds? Ruth gave him a spiral bound notebook, and he began to jot down notes in it despite the uncertainty that the words matched in any way what had mostly slipped away. The words were like the dregs at the bottom of a wine bottle that had set too long. They metastasized on their own, fermented, and threw out radiating rings of fungal growth reaching for a light that did not exist in this realm. To Sid, the words he wrote down had an incantatory power that matched that of his strange dreams. He realized that logic was a weak weapon as compared to the synergistic toxins of the mind leaching out through his fingers as he wrote. The more he wrote, the stronger the dreams became. But he could never remember them. They slipped away when he raised his head from the pillow. But then, in the middle of the day, he could see them, sometimes very clearly. He explained this to Ruth. By then it was August, and they were in the middle of a heat wave. And Ruth was tired, so very tired. She was losing patience with Sid. He had such a strong back and such a weak mind. The world was arranged in such a way that his options were limited. She tried to explain that to him, but Sid was having a hard time adjusting to the contingencies of daily living, never mind the unregimented proximity to other people.

"Look, I really feel it. I'm getting close to a breakthrough. I..."

"Sid, you can work at Market Basket and still write down your dreams."

"But sometimes they come to me late in the day."

"What are you trying to do? I know it was my idea to get you help. But really, do you think this is the way, Sid?"

"If just one person helps themselves, Ruth. It could save the world."

"You're such a big, strong guy. What are you gonna do when you're old?"

"What are you gonna do?"

"Hey. I've got a 401K with Pacha Mama."

"But how about Leesha?"

"She's on Medicaid."

"That's bullshit. She's not on Medicaid and you know it. You're not looking out for anyone. At least I take Leesha out to the park once in a while," said Sid, defensively.

"Leesha likes you," said Ruth, ruminating.

"Bullshit." said Sid.

"She told me. I know she likes you. Not like Jaydee. You didn't know him."

"Yeah," scoffed Sid. "The one with the treadmill. He didn't treat you very nice. Look how he took off for Arizona without you."

"You don't treat me very nice either, Sid."

"What do you mean? I do things for you here. And Rover's a good watch dog."

"Rover is useless."

"Sometimes I feel like beating the shit out of you," said Sid.

"If you even lay a finger on me it'll be the last thing you do," she growled.

When Sid and Ruth, both extra large, made love, the sofa tended to slide into the middle of the floor. This time one of the legs broke off. Rocking precariously, Sid muffled Ruth's mouth with his hand, and she bit him hard.

"Ow, " said Sid. Ruth began to laugh. It brought their lovemaking to a halt. When they were finished, lying in each other's arms in the doorway to the kitchen, they noticed that there was a strong smell of dogshit coming from the other side of the plywood island.

"Goddamned Rover," yelled Ruth. "I'm not cleaning it." She stood up.

"Sid, you need to get a job," she said. "Or get on disability."

"I don't know about that," said Sid.

Ruth nagged for several days, and finally Sid showered and walked up Loudon Road and past the airport to the Department of Health and Human Services offices mid-morning on a Thursday to try to get enrolled in some kind of program. He took a number and waited to see the woman through the window. She gave him a form to fill out. Sid didn't have a pen. He asked someone in line for a pen to fill out the form and sat at a long, fold-out table in the back. The metal seat legs reverberated loudly on the plastic floor as Sid shifted his weight to get a better look at the form, but nobody turned to look at him.

Some of the questions were troubling. He didn't even know what to write for former employment and thought Ruth could advise him as well as the woman in the window. So he folded the papers, stuck them in the back pocket of the green slacks of the correctional facility, and walked slowly past the airport and back down the hill, nursing his left foot with a slight limp. In the correctional facility there had been no hills to walk up or down. He tried to put the pain out of his mind, but it was constantly jumping up on him like Rover with demands for attention.

The waters of the Merrimack flowed under the bridge with a relentless power that soothed him, even as it reminded him of everything that was insurmountable in his life. If he looked back, if he cast himself back, there had been a child and seasons and adults that had struggled with forces that to the younger Sid had seemed distant but now were very visible. His father had not been a great parent. His mother had disappeared, but not before leaving an impression of regret and hunger running in her blood for generations. Along the banks, in the city land behind the ice arena, Sid could see the tents of the homeless. The encampment he could see through the trees, the plastic tarps dragging in the branches, were the aftermath, the leaf litter, of the storms that had pushed people out on a journey, when the Earth had still been young and beckoned with greater hope.

Regarding the paperwork, Ruth had an initial reaction of disappointment that reminded Sid of Yolanda, the way she would be overcome with dark moods when news came of his peccadilloes in high school, his attempts to win friends and earn the respect of the criminal element by defying norms and talking back to people. When he took out the folded and dinged up papers from his pocket, Ruth screeched. But they were just papers. They were meant to be mistreated.

"Look, Ruth," said Sid. "I don't think they're gonna help me much anyway."

"What are you talking about?"

"That's not what I need."

"What do you need, Sid?"

"I don't know."

"Well, while you figure it out, what about what I need? Some money for groceries would go a long way."

Ruth went about filling the boxes with information. For former employment, Ruth had him put down the laundry room of the correctional facility where Sid had for an indeterminate time folded sheets and stacked shelves with soap. She went online and found a name for the warden and wrote that down as a contact. She spelled out the name for Sid as she wrote. Sid watched her.

"Sid. There were dress codes for visitors. You couldn't wear see-through clothing of any kind. Did you get visitors, Sid?"

"Just once my brother came. That was a few years after I went in."

"I would have visited you. And I would have worn see-through clothing. Under my coat."

"You would have?"

"Why not? They have a problem with the female body?"

"I would have loved that."

"You didn't have much women?"

"No, not much."

"What was it like?"

"Yeah. I'd rather not talk about it."

"Did you have friends, Sid?"

"Not really, no."

"Why didn't your parents come to visit?"

"I don't know. I guess maybe they were ashamed of me."

"Aw, Sid. I'm sorry. They shouldn't have been. You were innocent."

"Yeah, maybe."

Sid didn't like talking about his past. Ruth tried to get as much out of him as she could, whenever he was unaware of providing information. She found out about Steve being an artist when they were going past the art supply store on Main Street.

"That's *The Flying Lovers,*" said Sid, pointing at the poster.

"How do you know?" asked Ruth.

"Steve told me."

Sid had learned about famous artists from his father. Steve had books of the artists he'd really admired, the abstract expressionists like Chagall and Kandinsky, who'd worked from subconscious forces in their lives by a process that ironically involved remembering dreams, just like Sid was doing.

Similarly, she learned that they'd used to raise chickens when Sid said something about the eggs she cracked into a bowl to make pancakes from scratch one Sunday morning.

"Those eggs look pale as shit. Not like the eggs we used to get," said Sid.

"Sid, where did you live? Before jail."

"Don't know, somewhere the fuck up north," said Sid. "Loonberg."

Ruth got on her phone after breakfast and started reading out the road names.

"Perley Hill Road. Sanborn Road. Needle Shop Road?"

"Nope, nope, nope. Just give up. It's useless. I don't remember squat," said Sid. He was lying on the floor playing with Rover, who had one of his boots in his mouth and was attempting to chew on it.

"Sid, we need to go up there and find it."

"Look, it's never going to be the same," Sid groaned.

"It's what it is. You go back, you find your house, your parents. It's a block in your brain, your memories, everything."

“You never tell me about you. What about your parents?” asked Sid.

“I told you. They live in Bedford. They’re divorced. My father works at Sam’s Club. My mother’s a para at the high school.”

“That’s so fuckin’ normal.”

“Right?”

“What about your old boyfriends? You never tell me, for example. Who’s Leesha’s father?”

“Leesha’s not even mine.”

“What?”

“Yeah. Her circumstances were very bad, Sid.”

“Wow.”

“I’ll tell you someday.”

“Wow.”

Sid looked at Leesha. She seemed to grimace, one eye dimming with sadness at some distant memory.

“Okay,” said Sid. “Let’s do it.”

“Do what now, Sid?”

“Go home. Loonberg.”

II - Loonberg

Lesli's car did very poor speed on the highway. Sid was driving. Ruth was in the back with Leesha and Rover. Lesli was in the passenger seat talking about a documentary she'd seen about the bees dying. The leaves were starting to turn on some of the trees. The radio was playing some rap music. Sid recognized the song. It reminded him of the hours every day in his bubble on the yard in the correctional facility. He wasn't listening to the conversation between Ruth and Lesli. They were getting passed by a lot of cars. Sid had settled into his role of chauffeur and was enjoying the view, listening to the music, and tending his memories, which for now were under control. He didn't like the noise the engine made, though, when they crested a rise. The car would pop and jolt them all. Lesli kept talking.

"Take this exit, Sid," said Lesli. She was using her phone for directions. Sid thought he recognized where he was.

They drove for a while through the forest. It was silent now, just Lesli telling Sid where to turn. Sid had turned off the radio when the reception deteriorated. They were on the back side of nowhere going up a steep climb on a road that looked like it was meant for off-road vehicles. The car shuddered as it dipped on one side in a rut.

"Are you guys sure this is right?" asked Ruth.

"Yeah, this looks like it," said Sid.

They came down a long winding hill lined with stone walls that were barely visible through sumac and knotweed. Houses began to appear. Some were old farm houses of moldering timbers up close to the road and some were newer dwellings set back in among the trees.

"This is it, " said Sid. "This is Loonberg."

He was excited by his sudden recognition of a place he'd grown up. He slowed the car down when he saw his old house, a modest colonial with a detached garage. It was painted a darker shade of brown. The garage looked different; maybe it had been rebuilt. But the windows in the house looked exactly the same. They had not changed. They were large, four of them, sixteen panes squared up along the front of the house. He remembered Yolanda and Steve arguing about the windows. They had been Steve's pride, he'd picked them up at an auction, but Yolanda had always complained about the wind getting through them. And the porch on the side overhanging the driveway was still there, only unpainted now, looking like it might take flight on its own. Sid idled along the road, just staring through the beech trees, the pale yellow leaves fluttering in the wind.

"We used to jump off there and do a flip into the snow, my brother and me," said Sid.

"Well, what are you going to do? Go see who's there. I'll go with you," said Ruth.

"What's the point?" asked Sid.

“Go on Sid,” said Lesli. “Just look around. Even if nobody’s there.”

Sid turned off the engine and climbed out, stepping onto the bank of dessicated brown ferns. Ruth got out of the back with Leesha.

“I’ll stay here with the dog,” said Lesli.

They walked back down the road to the driveway. Sid had an almost overpowering urge to check the mail in the mailbox. 331 Harlan Mill Road. They’d get letters, junk mail, and once in a blue moon a letter from Yolanda’s family out in Ohio.

“They changed the numbers. Used to be 16,” said Sid.

“There it is, Sid. Let’s go find out who lives there. Maybe your parents?”

“Yeah, somehow I doubt it.”

“You never know,” said Ruth.

Sid knocked on the door. He studied the cracking fibers in the clapboards of the exterior. There were potted plastic flowers on the porch that looked like they’d been there for years. The steps were covered in leaf litter. Ruth coughed and Leesha started to ask a question.

“Why does ...?”

“Shhh,” said Ruth, as the door creaked open.

A woman stared at them through the thin wedge of daylight spilling in from the outside. Sid could only see her eyes, and the gnarled tips of three fingers holding on the edge of the door. She said nothing.

"Hi there," said Sid. "I'm Sid Green. Grew up here. This was my house."

"Don't know. Can't help you there. Can't hardly hear," said the woman.

"I USED TO LIVE HERE. Do you remember Yolanda and Steve Green?" said Sid, clearing his beard away from his mouth.

"Yolanda and Steve who?"

"Green. They're the ones used to live here with me and my brother Darrell."

The door seemed to move, as if the woman was wavering, her thoughts unsure.

"We just want to check and make sure that this is the right house. Can we look around?" said Ruth, her voice exuding charm and good intentions.

"How do I know?" said the woman. She opened the door fully. She wasn't as old as she had first appeared in the slight initial crack of the door. She was about sixty, with thinning hair and a face wizened more from seclusion than exposure to the elements.

"Well, I used to live here," repeated Sid.

"I'm sorry for you," said the old woman.

"Who's there?" It was a voice from the back of the house.

"Oh," said the old woman. She was nervous and was about to shut the door. Sid stuck his foot out like he'd seen in the movies.

"My name's Sid," he said. "What's your name?"

"Oh. I'm... Jolene."

"Can we come in? She needs to use the bathroom," said Ruth, pointing at Leesha standing in front of her with a worried expression on her face.

"Of course, dear. Come in," said Jolene. She backed away from the door into the darkness of the house. Ruth pushed Leesha inside and turned to look at Sid with a stare and a nod that suggested he follow.

Once inside, Sid looked around. Everything looked oddly disjointed, as if his memories had been processed through a prism. Otherwise he was sure they were in the right place. The wallpaper was different. It was a floral pattern, aged and peeling in the corners of the wall. There were two sofas, cream colored, in the living room. He could see them around a corner of a wall, both rumpled and beaten. He remembered a distinctively handsome Chesterfield in leather that was missing along with the rustic chairs that Steve had made from cherry birch. And Jolene...he couldn't quite place her.

"Thanks, Jolene," said Ruth.

"Did you find the bathroom okay?" asked Jolene.

"Yes," said Leesha.

"Can we give you some water before you're on your way?" asked Jolene.

"What do you think, Sid? Water?" asked Ruth.

"No, that's fine. That was my bedroom, right there. And that was Darrell's down the hall," said Sid, stepping a few yards down the narrow entrance.

"Oh, no," said Jolene, worried. "You must be in the wrong house."

"How long have you lived here?" asked Sid.

"Oh my gosh. Forever," she said.

Creeping down the hall came an old man, pushing a cane out in front of him. His large head was full of neatly combed white hair, perched on a small, emaciated body. As he came into the living room, he stopped short with every step, using the cane to feel out in front of him. Ruth and Leesha stepped back.

"What is all this?" he asked.

"Dad. It's Sid, Dad," said Sid, heading into the living room towards the old man.

"Stop!" said the old man abruptly, holding the cane in the air.

Sid halted his careening lurch.

"Don't you remember me, Dad? It's Sid."

"Sid? I don't know a Sid," said the old man, disgustedly, spitting out the words.

"What are you talking about? I'm your son. Me and Darrell. Your two boys. Our Mom left when I was twelve. Then you married Yolanda. Remember?"

"I don't know what you're babbling about," said the old man. He caught his breath.

"They just showed up," said Jolene.

"God dammit. I've told you," said the old man.

"Dad, you must be Steve Green-Smith. The artist. Maybe you don't remember. Remember the wolf pack, Dad?"

The old man began to visibly shake. His face turned a bright red as the blood rushed to the skin.

"Get out! Now! Leave! I don't know who you are or what you want. But leave now or you will regret it!" he shouted.

"Aren't you Steve Green-Smith the artist?" groaned Sid.

"No! Never heard of him! Now leave!" said the old man, trembling with rage.

Leesha began to cry, her face silently contorting and tears squeezing from the corners of her eyes.

"Okay, Sid. That's all we can do," said Ruth, taking Sid's arm in both hands.

Leesha sobbed, tugging at Ruth's leg.

"You didn't tell me there was a child," said the old man. He moved with surprising agility around to the front door, blocking the exit.

"What's your name?" he asked, pointing his face in the direction of Leesha's stifled noises.

"I'm sure you don't need to know," said Ruth. "Come on, Sid, we're leaving," she added.

"I'm sorry I lost it just now. We don't get many visitors out here," said the old man.

"Ever since the flood," added Jolene.

"Well, you won't be seeing us again," said Ruth, pushing past the old man and out the door with Leesha.

Sid was stuck, he didn't know what to do. Steve had never been big on goodbyes. But this time it was different. There had been nineteen years of silence, and now it was as if he had never even existed.

"I understand, Dad. You're in pain. You just wanna forget. Just tell me where I can find Darrell," said Sid.

But the old man was unable to respond. Slumped against the wall, he slowly straightened and slipped away down into the darkness. The old woman watched Sid standing on the porch through a crack in the door.

Sid breathed deeply on the porch. He looked out towards the road. Many times in the past he and Darrell had walked out that door heading for a school bus waiting on the hill. Steve was always up and feeding the chickens or working in his workshop in the woods, feeding the woodstove with the firewood they seemed to spend half the summer splitting and stacking, the two boys and their father. How'd Steve get so old? What was the deal with all the denial? What did it matter anyway?

When they got back to the car, Sid seemed fine, although something about his silence seemed more brooding than usual. Ruth explained to Lesli that they'd found nothing in the house that definitely belonged to Sid or his family, except the two very odd older people who may or may not have been Sid's parents.

"Well, we can go to the town office and find out the names of the owners of the house," said Lesli, always practical.

"Great idea. What do you think, Sid?" said Ruth.

"It doesn't matter. Don't you think I'd recognize my own father?"

“Yeah, but why would he refuse to admit it?” asked Ruth.

“Really,” said Lesli.

“Who cares? He might have a good reason. Knowing Steve, it probably has something to do with his artistic career. He was always doing things that made no sense to anybody else.”

“Well. There’s always the town clerk. You feel like going there, Sid?” asked Lesli.

“I can’t drive,” said Sid.

“Let’s switch,” said Lesli.

Sid slumped in the back seat with Rover at his feet, inconsolably sunk in thought, while Lesli drove them through a dizzying series of twists and drops. They came out onto a paved road that went past a river, spilling over the banks of an old mill. Up the hill was the town of Loonberg, a bank, a gasoline station, what had once been the town store -- Loonberg Corners in fading paint on the sign attached to the side of the building -- and a church with a tottering steeple that also housed the town library and town clerk’s office. It was painted a distinctly unchurchlike shade of purple, an irreverent touch in the dilapidated intersection.

Lesli parked in the gas station. They all got out slowly and stretched. It didn’t seem like a great place to find any answers. They waited to cross the street at the stop sign. A truck rolled through the stop sign, crossed the intersection, and stopped in front of the convenience store. A man got out of the truck, its engine still running, and went inside the store. As they crossed the street, Sid could hear the rumble of falling water coming from the river behind the church.

It's night again. The fire going in the old fireplace is roaring into life as he pokes at it with something. He turns and looks at you and walks over to the hearth. He wants to show you something, so you follow. The flames of the fire are licking at the air, as if trying to reach beyond the invisible border of the hearth. It's a portrait, an old yellowed photograph of a woman in a brown leather frame. He holds it out to you. You refuse to take it. You know who she is. You've heard the story before. Now is not the time. Outside it is snowing. You can sense the cold by the way the fire is roaring. He begins:

"She was the one who wanted the gold. She loved you but she sent you on your way to find me. It took you three months to sail from Liverpool to Cape Town and once there you signed on with Colquhoun and were taken on one of the artillery guns in the company that had formed for the great march inland. The train's terminus in those days was Bulawayo. You didn't know where I was, but you'd heard there were concessions and you thought it was likely that I would be found.

You were a good man for the figures. They put you in charge of the company's administration in the Matabeleland. You had a home there. It was called the Queen's Mine. There was a deposit of tin. It overlooked the ridged and ancient countryside. A big man you were then, and you forgot about your home in Leitrim. But you couldn't forget about me. You'd heard stories of the white man who had amassed quite a fortune trading with the Portuguese up country. You had heard he was known as a friend of Umtasa, that he was living in the kraal of Umtasa and had taken on a wife among Umtasa's people. You decided you needed to see for yourself.

In the night you gathered provisions and cleaned your rifle. The Mauser fired a smokeless cartridge but it needed a meticulously clean barrel and chamber. You enjoyed breaking it down in the light of the oil lamp at the big table in your study. The garden boy, Mjebe brought you a glass from the kitchen and you instructed him to pour from the bottle of English gin that you had on the windowsill. He did so and left the glass on the windowsill. He stood there watching you, just on the edge of your vision.

'You can go now, Mjebe,' you said. You wanted to be left alone. You were thinking about me, conjuring memories like a hunter. But the boy refused to go. He wanted a favor.

'Before you go to Umtasa, sir, I want to know if you can pay for a white doctor for my mother. She is very sick, tenzi.'

'You don't trust the bush medicine?'

'No.'

'Well, then. Of course. When I come back.'

'No. This night, sir.'

'Why?'

'Because you will die, sir.'

'Why? How do you know?'

'I feel it.'

'Then you will come with me to prevent it from happening.'

'But I can't leave her, sir.'

'Of course you can, and you will, Mjebe. You'll come with me. In the morning. We'll take two of the pack ponies.'

You struck through the bush country for three days, going north to Lake Kariba. It was dry and hot and you found the going slow. Mjebe complained constantly. He was unsuited for the trek. On the second morning you shot an eland at a watering hole and cut the joints and some of the meat off the shoulder, leaving the rest for the hyenas. You packed the meat in a swath of linen. At night you stopped and unloaded the tents from the ponies in a hollow of the veld. You lit a fire and cooked the strips of meat on spits. Mjebe lay down and slept, drowsy after the meal, but you stayed awake and watched the stars for hours. You were thinking of me and of her. In the night, in your dreams, we were together, playing with the greyhounds on the tiled floor in the kitchen of Teach Léin. Then in the morning, in the first light, you thought you could see the lake shimmering in the distance on the far western edge of the horizon. By the afternoon of that day, you were approaching Umtasa's compound. Despite a full belly the night before, you were hungry. Mjebe was threatening to run away back to the mine. You had few certainties left aside from the slog of the ponies as they sensed water, the buzz of the flies, and the silence that lay festering everywhere between you and the world.

The town offices were open half a day Mondays and Thursdays, the man in the general store said. He rang up the bottle of iced tea for Ruth, while Lesli studied the trinkets on the rotating display next to the door. Leesha took the bottle and tried to open it herself before Ruth got her change on the ten dollar bill. Sid took the bottle and twisted off the cap for her. Outside, the trucker started up his diesel engine and made his way out on the road again.

"What are you looking to do in town?" asked the man, suddenly talkative and smiling.

"Well, Sid here grew up here," said Ruth.

Sid turned around and smiled back at the store clerk.

"You probably don't remember me," said Sid. "I lived out on Harlan Mill Road. I used to stop in before getting on the bus in high school," said Sid.

"Well, you've grown a little since then," said the man. He almost smiled.

Sid laughed a small chuckle. "Yeah. Probably."

The store clerk stroked his beard.

"Steve Green-Smith. Remember him?" asked Sid.

"Of course," said the man. "He was a bit of a crank. Was he something to you?"

"Yes."

"Didn't know he had any family. Why don't you try the Rock and Bark camp down on Wappinger Meadow? That's where a lot of the folks around here end up when they get tired of paying their taxes."

"Yeah, he had two kids. Me and my brother Darrell."

"Don't think I'd heard that part of the story," said the man.

The Rock and Bark camp announced its presence with a Gadsden flag attached to an erratic the size of a house. They parked on the edge of a swamp, a rime of ice within a few feet of the tires. Above the erratic, among the hemlocks, were scattered Winnebagos, and dilapidated sheds spilled plastic snow shovels, tarpaulins, rusted propane tanks, and other accouterments of summers past that had stretched into fall and lately, for a few scofflaws, into a year-round refuge from the brutality of pilgrim lands.

Lesli, Ruth, and Sid walked into the camp, looking around for signs of life. Leesha stayed with Rover in the car. She was getting hungry. Sid was in favor of heading out to the highway again and stopping at a pizza place he remembered in Laconia. There was an old barn cat circling in front of a parked car. Smoke curled from the tin stove pipe at the apex of a moss-covered roof. A door cracked open and a woman stumbled out, followed by a black man. They both laughed. Inside the house, a woman screamed. The door slammed shut with a muffled whap as if the house was full. The man and woman stopped when they saw Lesli, Ruth and Sid moseying in the camp entrance. The man leaned against the car and the woman stopped and blew her nose, one nostril at a time, on the ground. Sid strode over to them slowly, drawn by the languid way they moved, as if there was nothing better coming their way that day. But he suddenly shivered and drew up his shoulders. The woman stared at him and dropped her hands from her face.

“Excuse me,” said Sid.

“Yo,” said the man.

Sid stared hard, studying their features, the black man’s relaxed arms and legs, the woman’s brown hair pinned behind small ears.

“Don’t I know you?” said the woman, stepping up to Sid.

“Maybe,” he said.

The wispy curls of her mid-length hair, the precise curve of her waist, all suggested something important to Sid, something that he needed to remember, that he had blocked and denied. He scowled, trying hard to think. The woman exclaimed suddenly, a perturbed yell that stood up the hair on Sid’s neck.

“Why’d you come back? You think you can come back here just like that?”

“I…”

“You killed her, Sid. I can never forgive you.”

“Meg?”

“No,” said the woman.

“I didn’t kill her,” said Sid.

“You’re always lying. Is that why you’re here? To finish the job?”

“What’s up, Melissa?” asked the black man, straightening from the car.

“I didn’t kill her. She hit her head on a rock when the boat turned over and drowned.”

"You killed her and dumped the body in the fucking river to make it look like a drowning."

"No," said Sid.

"She had the marks! I don't know what he's doing back here," she said.

The black man looked at Sid, and made a smacking sound with his mouth.

"Maybe you should go," he said. Sid leaned back, about to lunge at him, but Ruth and Lesli grabbed an arm each.

"Sid!" said Ruth.

The two women hanging on his arms were the counterweights to his madness. He took to his knees.

"I didn't kill her," he said, covering his head with his hands. "All these years I knew it. But nobody believed me. Nobody."

"Come on, Sid," said Ruth, stroking his broad back as if he were a dog.

"If you need it, we got a place for y'all," said the black man.

"Sid, are you okay?" asked Ruth.

"I don't know," he said.

"Look, it's not great, but it's a place. You can have it for as long as you need," said the black man. "My name's Phil, by the way. Philadelphia Collins."

"I'm Lesli Burdick," said Lesli, craning her neck to look up at him. "And that's Ruth Rendell. And he's Sid. I don't know his last name."

"Yo," said Phil.

“Sid Green,” said Melissa, spitting on the ground. “I don’t know what you think you’re doing, but you’re aiding a fucking criminal,” she added, stepping up to Ruth and Lesli.

“Sid’s a good man,” said Ruth. “He’s paid his dues. You need to get off his case.”

“He killed my sister,” said Melissa.

The two women stared at each other and swayed like cobras.

“Back off, Ruth,” said Lesli.

Sid slowly stood, dazed by the proceedings. He meandered towards the entrance, crossed over the road to where the culvert let water flow into a canal. He watched the water hit on the rocks at the bottom of the culvert as if there was a clue to be found for what was happening in his life, what had happened, what could never unhappen, as if there was a break he could find in the fabric of reality. He heard Rover barking inside the car. Leesha stared at him from the back, her face against the glass. Her calm, questioning gaze stilled Sid’s heaving heap of a mind. He went to the car and opened the door.

“Are we going home, Sid?” asked Leesha.

“No. We’re going to stay here awhile, Leesh,” he said. She crawled out of the door into his arms. Rover jumped out and ran down the road barking.

The dilapidated old building the size of a garden shed was higher up on the hill, under a grove of hemlock trees which kept it in the shade. The wet stoop up to the door bent dangerously under their weight. The door was open. Ruth and Lesli were already inside arguing about something. Sid strained to hear what they were saying. He put Leesha down on the ground, and she ran up the stoop awkwardly and inside the cabin.

"Yo, there you go, brother." said Phil from behind him.

"Sorry about what happened back there," said Sid, turning around in the door, studying the black man's face.

"No problem. We're here to help folks outs who's in trouble. You can just chill here as long as you want. We'll talk money later."

Ruth looked up from her spot at a small sink, running the brown, tepid water. She turned off the water, held out a glass for Leesha. She kept Leesha against her legs while she drank. Sid stood in the doorway, blocking it entirely with his massive frame, studying the scene. He couldn't make sense of it. Lesli came up to him.

"Sid, how do you feel about staying?" she said.

"Only if you want it, Sid. You can come back with us today," said Ruth.

"I don't know," said Sid.

"Stay here for a while, Sid. I think it'll be good for you," said Lesli.

"I'm not so sure," said Ruth. "This shit is fucking weird, Sid."

"Everything's weird, Ruth," said Sid.

"That's what I think," said Lesli. "There's something here for you. I'm not sure what it is, but you can stay as far as Phil is concerned, so why not, right? I'm working tonight. I'll be in the car," she added, turning to Ruth. Smiling, she hugged Sid, looked him briefly in the eye, and went out the door.

"What do you think, Leesha? Do you want Sid to come back with us?" asked Ruth.

"I want Sid to be happy," said Leesha.

"That's what we all want," said Ruth.

"Wow," said Sid.

"Is that what you want, Sid?"

What Sid wanted was to put a hold on the water spilling downstream. If he could only run back again through the past, the black mouth of nothingness that had blanked him out, leaving the wind in the trees and the voices in his head. Sid wanted to score a touchdown to erase all the past. But he needed to find the plumb line of the playing field.

"I want someone to believe me for once," said Sid.

"I believe you," said Ruth.

"That's why I love you, Ruth," said Sid.

"Someday, baby. But I need to get back to pay the rent," said Ruth.

They sat together on the motley old sofa. Ruth leaned against him and Leesha lay down across their laps. Sid could hear Rover barking somewhere outside.

"How long do you think I should stay here?" asked Sid.

"As long as you want, Sid. There's nobody in this place at this time of year."

"I guess I'll stay for a couple a days, Ruth."

"You stay and find out as much as you can about yourself, Sid. I'll be back in a couple of days, and then we'll go to the Market Basket and talk to the people there about getting you a job."

"Okay. Help me get Rover in here before you go."

"We'll get his bag of food and the sandwiches in the car."

Sid walked back down the hill with Ruth and Leesha. Rover came running up the road from the swamp and tried to jump back in the car when they opened the door. Sid grabbed him and picked him up in his arms. The dog squirmed his body around and scratched at Sid with his hind legs. Sid watched the back of the car as it drove away with Rover laying still now in his arms and the bag of dog food and sandwiches at his feet. Leesha turned around. Her parting gaze was a question for him.

The camp was empty, just the smoke curling from the roof of the main house. Mostly, the seasonal residents all seemed to have left. Sid walked back up the hill with Rover in his arms and deposited him on the stoop. Rover ambled inside, sniffing, and Sid closed the door behind him, satisfied. Rover scratched at it. Sid stood on the wet stoop and looked out at the camp. He felt oddly at peace, as if he had landed suddenly in a place from which he could not easily be moved by events or natural circumstances. What he could discern momentarily, like the sighting of a long absent friend in the distance, in some crowd on a city street, was a sense of himself from an internal sensor that had been silenced sometime in the last nineteen years by pain medication and the blunt force trauma of incarceration. He let Rover out, and they went up the road past the last of the vacated summer sheds, Sid striding slowly and the dog bounding ahead and stopping to wait.

Sid headed off on a narrow mud track that led along a fence line and ended in a pile of brush and leaves on the edge of the woods. The road wound back down on the other side of the sheds. He called Rover, keeping the dog near him as they bushwhacked through a thick grove of birch saplings. Sid's old, oversized boots sank in the sodden debris of fallen leaves.

The second growth forest yielded no answers. Sid felt his heart pumping harder, out of sync, when he stopped and sat on a log in a clearing. There were downed trees, jagged stumps and piles of branches all around. Sid sat in the middle of a cut-over lot. Blackberry vines and sumac saplings had established their healing presence just before the cold had set in and the summer had slunk away to nurse its wounds. As the sun sank below the tree line, Sid reached inside his own mind and found no answer. Despite the lack of bars or even walls, he was no better off than before. There were gunshots firing in the distance. There was nothing inside or out that pointed the way to freedom. In the lengthening shadows lay a thinly veiled threat of violence.

Sid found himself lost on the back side of the swamp as the twilight descended. He came out in a clearing over an old beaver dam and thought there might be a road ahead through the woods, but there hadn't been one. An old stone wall demarcated the foundations and cellar hole of an ancient dwelling, and a few hundred yards on Sid walked through a lost burial ground with toppled and careening gravestones, their inscriptions mostly rubbed out and illegible. It was almost dark by the time he stumbled over a rise to an old logging road. On the opposite edge, amid brown ferns, a hunter in an orange cap hunched over a deer carcass. Rover growled deep in his throat. Sid stopped and quieted him. The hunter looked up and greeted him with a stare.

"How goes it?" Sid asked as he crouched along the road, pulling Rover by the scruff of the neck.

"Not too bad," said the man, half hidden in the trees.

"Good luck with that," said Sid.

"Thanks," said the hunter.

Sid looked at the hunter's face and thought he recognized him from some well of the past. He found himself back to the Rock and Bark camp along the rutted backroads, trusting his intuitions and memories as to directions, and Rover stayed by him in the dark, too afraid to wander. When he saw the fire arcing in the distance and heard the distant voices, coming onto the long, twisting downhill stretch of road to the swamp, Sid realized his wet feet were in pain. He hadn't thought of his feet as separate from the rest of his body. He saw them now as victims, products of neglect, worthy of compassion, and felt sorry for the way that he had been treating them. Along with Rover, his feet were his only responsibility now, and he realized he had been heedless of them for far too long.

Sid ate a couple sandwiches in the shed with his boots off. It was cold and lonely, even with Rover, who chowed on the dry dog food pellets that Sid poured out in a small neat pile on the floor.

“Good boy,” said Sid. His own voice in the cabin sounded strange to his ears.

He rinsed his mouth and washed his face and hair with water from the sink tap. The sink was clogged. He tried to get it to drain by using his hand as a plunger, and eventually that worked. He dried with a rag hanging on the windowsill and put back on the damp Goodwill tee shirt he’d been wearing, the sweatshirt over it with the Jack Daniels logo, and pulled on the two pairs of sweat socks and the boots. Then he went out to warm up by the fire and find something to help him sleep through the cold night. He left Rover inside. Rover whined behind the door.

The fire was burning scrap wood, cardboard, and some wet, half-rotted pallets stacked at the edge of the yard. There was a car coming around the bend on the road, and the people around the fire, some in lawn chairs, others standing, watched the car go behind the rock and emerge on the other side to continue steadily increasing speed up the hill.

“Cops,” said a woman across the fire.

“They're fine. We have an understanding. Nobody’s supposed to be here, but as long as they get names, a complete list of the registered guests with home addresses, they’re fine. Adams paid up with the select board and nobody getting hurt,” said Phil.

Sid joined the circle, standing next to two guys in baseball caps and Carhart coats passing a pipe. One of them offered up the pipe to Sid, who waved it away.

“Who’s Adams,” Sid asked.

"Phil, who's Adams?" asked one of the men in Carharts next to Sid, relaying his question.

"Adams is the landlord," said Phil. "Whyn't we go around and introduce ourselves? We got some new people here who need to know stuff. We'll start with names and why you here."

"I don't know why I'm here," cackled the woman, coughing and hacking into the flames on the opposite side to Sid. Somebody threw a ragged, punky length of two by six into the pit. The fire jumped in response.

"I'll start us off then. My name's Phil Collins. Some people call me Philadelphia."

"Hey, Phil Collins," said one of the guys next to Sid, elbowing his partner. "I never thought of that."

"Yeah, genius," said Phil. "I was Phil Collins long before you ever heard of that other Phil Collins."

That seemed to quiet things down. The flames licked higher. Ribs on a pallet turned red and racked.

"Anyway, I'm here because me and Sylvia was evicted three years ago near to the day. From the Tanglewood Estates in Colebrook 'cause we missed half a month rent. 'Cause Sylvia got her ass fired from Michaels for shoplifting some ribbons. Sylvia? You got anything?"

Sylvia, the older woman across the fire from Sid, coughed and hacked into the fire again before speaking.

"You're here because I put up with the fact you never paid a bill in ya life that you could stiff on and the fact that, if you were in

Lawrence right now you'd be dead because you stole business off Carlos Corona."

"Yeah, okay. True that part," said Phil.

"And I'm here … because it's okay to get high here," concluded Sylvia.

"That's right. Let's not forget that," said somebody.

Another woman sitting in a lawn chair, wrapped in a blanket, stirred. Sid studied her face in the firelight.

"Better than Elm Street," added Sylvia.

"Fucken straight," said one of the Carhart coats. His partner sniggered.

It was quiet for a long time. Sid studied the fire reflected in the bizarre, dancing faces of the people around it. It was Melissa, Meg's sister, wrapped in a blanket and slumped in a lawn chair. She would not look up despite Sid staring hard at her. Then Sid sensed the guy next to him tense, wanting to take his turn speaking out.

"Hey, I'm Jeff and this is Dylan," said the Carhart guy.

"Yay, Jeff. And Dylan, too," said Phil.

" And we're here because we heard it was an awesome place on a weeknight with good people and good music. What happened to the music? Oh, and just the sick shit we like to share with people who like to party."

"You're welcome here," said Phil. "We work with all kinds."

"No music," said Sid, feeling sassy suddenly. "Fuck that."

There was a muffled, solid chuckle out of Dylan.

"Let's hear from you, chief. You a new face here," said Phil.

Sid looked around the fire, stage struck.

"I don't know lots of you people here. I grew up in Loonberg," said Sid.

"Loonberg sucks," said Jeff.

"Cops in Loonberg suck. People are okay," said Phil, correcting him.

"What's your name?" asked Sylvia.

"I was away for nineteen years," said Sid, ignoring her.

"Loony tunes tryin' a find out where all the good folks in Loonberg went," said Phil. "World's changed and shit on him. We can help you, man. Deal with the change. It's called medication."

Dylan laughed. Sid decided to ignore the taunts and, like his president, soldier on to the end.

"I was innocent. Innocent. Never touched her. Always loved her."

"Yeah, Sid. You were just perfect, my ass. I knew you back when you were just a kid, Sid. I knew you when you were just a little shit on the Ferncroft playground sniffin' glue, which fucked you up. As a matter of fact, I don't know how you avoided juvie. Oh, yeah. Football." Melissa spit on the ground beside the lawn chair disgustedly.

"Meg liked hanging out with you because you were fun. She would have lost interest in you eventually, I'm sure of that. But you never gave her the chance, did you?"

Melissa sat up in the lawn chair and shook off the blanket onto the ground. She wiped her hands on her knees and rubbed them together, holding them out to the fire.

"God knows I didn't kill her."

"God don't know shit," said Melissa, bounding to the fire and glaring across it to Sid.

"Hey, lay off him," said Sylvia. "That's out of bounds. A little respect around here. He says he didn't do it. So he didn't do it."

"Yeah, leave God out of it," said Jeff.

Sid stared hard at Melissa, into her eyes, and couldn't help seeing Meg in her. Meg, the golden girl, the valedictorian. Meg, who'd owned a horse and been a cross country skier from the age of five. She had loved everything they did together, making love in his car and blacking out on the bottle of Wild Irish Rose he stole from the general store in town, her breasts shaking when she laughed, arching her back in the dark; then skipping classes in the spring of senior year and driving the long back roads across the forests of Coos to Quebec. They almost didn't get back in because Sid's birth certificate was a barely legible copy he'd made the day before in the school library. The border agents had relented with them, the evil spawn best kept at home, high on a cocktail of coke, weed, acid, and all manner of natural toxins, letting them back in at Rock Island. Meg still felt like a ghost part of him: the razor cutting, the pangs in his head, heart, and stomach. Even his knees buckled when he thought of her on the riverbank, her face swollen and twisted like a pallet board in the fire.

It was dark in Phil's house except for the lights from the wireless speaker on the sink that blared a rumbling mix of hip hop and techno. There were people on the floor and on two easy chairs, and there were glints of lighters and the sound of voices, and then the barely audible gasps as the mainline spiked. Sid watched his arm as Melissa knotted the surgical tubing around it, pulling it quite tight. Sid clenched his fist.

"What are you trying to prove, Sid? You're one of us?" she asked, licking the end of the hypodermic as it spurted out a drop of the warmed up brown liquid.

"Shut up," said Sid. He didn't want to hear anything. He wanted all the voices stilled, forever. Melissa accommodated him. She poked the needle into his vein and pushed the poison inside.

The times Sid had gotten lost in the woods, it was always Darrell that was sent out to find him. Sid could hear his brother's steps crunching on fresh snow. He swore that there were animals that had kept him alive with their breath. Darrell was never angry at him when he tried to explain that dying was not the worst thing that could happen to them. Darrell was just that much younger that he could never understand what Sid was saying, and besides, Sid had proved that he was wrong so many times. He couldn't blame Darrell for not understanding. Darrell always managed to drag him home to Steve, though.

The board, smoothly worn by years of use, would come off its hook on the back door. Steve would take him by the wrist and lead him to the workshop. In later years he would command Sid to lean against the outside wall of the shop and grab onto the windowsill. Sid's fingers would curl and turn white. He remembered his pale white, disconnected fingers when Steve was done. He couldn't feel anything in his hands as the blood drained and pooled into his feet, the large feet that held him up like angular stands as he swayed, lost consciousness and slumped against the back door, Darrell watching secretly from the pantry window and Yolanda in the living room reading her magazines, pretending that everybody was fine.

"You're never going to find her. You're never getting her back. You're stuck here with us now, Sid."

It was Melissa. She was making love to him in some strange way with her eyes. Sid was looking up at her. She leaned over him. They were on the floor. He was alive, and Rover was barking. It was day now, and Sid sat up and rubbed his face. Rover circled, hungry, sniffing in the air. Melissa was gone. She had just been there, but now she was gone. Sid ran the sink and stuck his face under the cold water, slapped and rubbed it all over his face and chest as Rover watched. Afterwards, he dried off with the Goodwill tee shirt and put the sweatshirt back on with his correctional facility pants. He tried massaging his feet. They hurt, worse than before. He put back on his damp socks and boots. He had not moved on the journey through the maze of his mind and back again. It might have been for a couple of days, it might have been a week. But somebody must have come and let Rover out, somehow he must have gotten to the toilet. There was snow on the ground, already disappearing as the sun cleared out a bank of clouds above the hemlocks. Rover barked.

"Shut up," said Sid. He felt like his body would collapse like a sack of jelly if exposed for more than a few seconds to daylight, his stomach convulsing in rebellion. If he didn't eat, it would only get worse as his body readjusted to the passage of time. Either way it would be bad, but it was better to try and get some food into his stomach. He walked down the hill, shaking his head to get it to stop spinning. Rover ran along beside him, sniffing and falling back. Sid went out on the road, past the erratic crowned with the coiled snake, the flag motionless in the middle of a grey sky.

The door slammed. Sid turned and saw Phil stumbling out of the main house, smoke shooting from the tin pipe in the roof, buttoning his pants as he came down the snow-coated path, his legs working crazily.

"Hey. Yo. Where you going, brother?"

Sid stopped. Rover barked and ran over to Phil, jumping up on him in greeting.

"Where in the hell you going?" Phil stopped in front of him, pushed Rover down, and settled things in his crotch.

"Up to town. Get some food," said Sid. "It's a free country."

"We got food. Come get you some pancakes," said Phil.

Sid watched him. The words didn't match his face.

"Pancakes and a slab of bacon," said Phil. "Come on, chief. You can't go up to town like that. Get this fucking dog away."

"Come here, Rover," said Sid.

Phil sighed.

"You got coffee?" asked Sid, bending down and scratching Rover's ears.

"Of course I got coffee."

"I'm kind of messed up without coffee," said Sid.

"Know about that shit. Once you get feelin' straight I got a deal for you. Come on in, though."

Inside the main house was warm from the fire. Sylvia, the old woman from the fire, sat at the folding table in the hall off the kitchen. Sid could see the pot of coffee on the sill and the frying pan on the electric griddle.

"Sylvia," said Phil. "You know Sid, right?"

"Yeah, how are you, Sid? Feeling better?"

"Not really," said Sid.

"Need a doctor?" asked Sylvia.

"I don't think so," said Sid.

"Nothing some breakfast and coffee can't fix," said Phil. "Have a seat, brother."

Sid sat down. Rover barked and whined outside the door. Sylvia put aside her book and took off her reading glasses.

The old woman reminded him of his former art teacher, Mrs. DeLeone in high school who'd thought he had artistic potential. She'd encouraged him to get the football scholarship to UNH so he could continue his art and drawing classes and get a degree and be a teacher like her. But Sid had known he was never going to be an artist like Steve or a teacher like Mrs. DeLeone. And he'd grown tired of it all, tired of football. Instead, he'd looked into and applied for ROTC. The problem had been his flat feet. It had looked to Sid that spring like he was going to have to keep playing, keep battering heads as an outside linebacker and fullback, even though he hated the game, hated the hype, hated the way it made people call him the "two-way threat" in the Daily Sun. The only person he could talk to about his real feelings, his desires for a different sort of life, a different sort of man he could inhabit, had been Meg. And she was dead. But her face, swollen and twisted in the sun, the last memory he had of her, was that all that was left? He didn't believe in God, not the God of the Bible who was a very glorified accountant, as far as he could tell, keeping track of the ledger of sins for everyone. A very busy man. He didn't know what he believed. But there was something. It lay behind the days like a coiled snake waiting to spit out its venomous truth when you stumbled, when you were down, least expecting it. Many days Sid had lain in his cell, snake bit, and now he remembered.

Phil was busy mixing up some batter in a bowl and heating up the griddle. Sid looked around nervously. Phil set down a mug in front of him and poured it full of steaming coffee.

"Sugar?" asked Sylvia, pushing the bowl of packets over to him.

"Sure," said Sid, grabbing a couple of Sweet and Lows awkwardly with frozen fingers and using his teeth to tear them open. Phil poured in some milk out of an old carton. Sid swirled the milk and dust around in the mug of black coffee until they disappeared.

Pancakes and bacon fried in the griddle. Sid thought he should measure his words carefully even as his body thawed with the warm food. It was all he had going for him, the ability to marshal and ration his thoughts.

Sylvia vacated her seat. Phil sat opposite him and watched as he ate.

"Good, huh?"

"Yeah," said Sid, chewing voraciously.

"You're probably wondering why you're here, huh? Is that right?"

"Yeah," said Sid.

"These women ain't coming back, don't look like," said Phil.

"Never know," said Sid. "She probably will. How many days it been?"

"Shit. Been like five days, man. You've been out like a log. I been comin in and lookin after that dog, Sid."

"Rover thanks you."

"Yeah, well I need a favor from you, especially seeing as how I never gonna be getting the rent that woman promised."

"Sure. Maybe. What do you need?"

"Well, I don't have to tell you you're built, Sid. You set up like you could do some work, right?"

"Well, what kind of work?"

"I have a friend who needs some help around his place with some projects he got. He's always looking for somebody reliable and discreet, if you know what I mean. Imma set you up with him, Sid. Take you up there this afternoon if you feelin right."

Sid was quiet, chewing the food and looking down at the table.

"This could be a great opportunity for you, Sid. This guy is rich as shit, man."

"Okie doke. We'll check it out."

"Check it out. That's right. More eggs? How 'bout some coffee, Sid?"

Sid was thankful for the food and the fact that his hunger made it feel like his body was functioning normally. By the afternoon he felt capable enough to go for a walk with Rover, and he planned to set out again into the woods from the shed at the top of the hill. As he started to rouse himself from the rumpled, foam-leaking sofa, he heard knocking at the door, and then Phil opened and let himself in.

"You feelin' better, Sid?"

"Yeah, I think so."

"Let's go then. We gotta go now, while it's still hot. Bernier, the guy I told you about? He's here. Usually, he could be anywhere. He flies his own airplane. He has a whole fucking airforce, man."

"Well, can Rover come?"

"Sure, bring Rover. Just keep him under control."

"Rover's a good boy."

"Yeah, all right, Sid."

Phil had a truck, an old Ram, that had some issues. He had a box of tools out on the snow. Sid grudgingly pitched in to help out. He looked at the spark plugs and cleaned the gaps out with some sandpaper while Phil was talking. He sprayed some carb cleaner down into the cylinders.

"Hey, you know 'bout snowmobile engines?" asked Phil.

"Sure, we always kept a couple of them around the place," said Sid.

The Ram fired up after a couple of tries. Phil mumbled something about the battery. Sid made sure Rover was settled comfortably at his feet.

"Are you looking to buy a Skidoo or something?" asked Sid, making conversation.

"Maybe," said Phil.

They drove for about an hour, along back roads and then a couple of exits on the highway. The house was up a mile-long driveway, almost at the top of a mountain. It looked out over Winnipisaukee and the North Country. The mountains across the lake had a cover of white on them. Sid was concentrating on his body, trying to keep from feeling any pain with all the jolts of the road in the old truck with the worn suspension. He was feeling sorry for himself a lot also, thinking of Ruth and Leesha and the fact that Ruth seemed to have dumped him. Partly, his feelings were due to coming down off the drugs. He knew it could be withdrawal symptoms, and perhaps Ruth was just then on her way to the Rock and Bark to pick him up and bring him back to Concord. He would never know because he didn't have a phone or a way of contacting her. He didn't even have a number for her. It made him feel like he was failing. And now this, the long driveway and the log-house mansion at the top of the clearcut, with the spectacular view. It didn't seem like the opening of a happy chapter in his life. Phil was very quiet and focused.

They parked in a spot in the snow marked for the purpose by a half-buried utility pole, stained dark with creosote.

"Stay here," said Phil.

Sid watched him walk across the ice on the wide driveway that led around to the multi-level log house and large barn, with doors that slid on metal tracks mounted on the outside wall. A couple of men stood on the cement slab of the open barn, dressed in coats and baseball caps, holding phones down on their bellies. They looked up at Phil. He waved and they merely swayed where they were, like strands of seaweed, moored to an ocean floor of duty and hidden vocations. Phil talked to them, moving uncertainly, swaggering, his hands motioning back and forth to the two men as if he were dispensing favors. Then one of the men followed Phil back to the car. Sid grabbed Rover in his arms and opened the door. He stepped out into the sunlight. The air was crisp up here, cooler by a few degrees than it had been at the Rock and Bark. Breath came out in billows of condensation. Sid squinted as Phil approached with the guy in the ballcap, hands in the pockets of the black coat.

They were both silent.

"Hey," said Sid. "Be a good boy." Rover was squirming in his arms. He put him down. Rover barked and circled around behind Phil and the black coat. The man turned and watched Rover carefully, never taking his hands out of his pockets. Sid concluded he had a gun in there.

"We're going in now, Sid. Meet Bernier hisself."

"Okay."

"What about the dog?" said the black coat.

"He's coming with me. Come here, Rover," said Sid.

Rover came back to Sid and sat by his side. Sid kneeled in the snow, patting his head and whispering to him.

"Good boy, Rover," said Sid, standing.

They stood there. The black coat was on the phone for a while with his back to them. The wind made it hard to hear what he was saying. Phil awkwardly shifted his weight from foot to foot. Rover circled around and around the car yard in wider orbits, sniffing the ground, looking up occasionally to see Sid watching. Then the black coat mumbled something. With his hands in his pockets again, he started walking away. Phil followed and nodded his head at Sid for him to do the same. Sid stood. He and the dog walked behind the two men over to the mansion.

The front entrance consisted of wide, neatly cut stone steps. Three of them. Then the front door opened. A young Asian guy in a camel hair sportcoat and an odd, lopsided haircut held the door and watched them come in, looking disapprovingly at Sid, the last one in, holding Rover by the scruff. Sid looked up as he walked and let

Rover go. A massive, log-beamed cathedral ceiling and skylights arched over the interior. The walls were hung with stuffed trophies of horned game animals - moose, elk, and mountain sheep. The black coated man walked across the tiled foyer to a glass elevator shaft and stopped. Phil, Sid, and the dog caught up to him. The elevator doors opened. Sid held it open with his shoulder and called softly for Rover. The dog trotted in and the elevator doors closed. They rose to the top floor.

Bernier's office was in a bedroom down a hallway and around a couple of bends. A gable window looked out over the snow-capped mountains. The hum of soft mood music, forest soundscapes, came from somewhere. Bernier was at a laptop, reclining against the antique wooden headboard of the king-size bed. A woman sat on the bed also, reading a book. Bernier was a twenty something, with a handlebar moustache and moussed hair, a blond wave on his forehead. The woman, a redhead, older than Bernier, kept her legs in jeans like bent toothpicks beneath her and her shoulders covered in some Mexican looking wrap. When Bernier saw Phil, a smile crept over his face, the smile of a practiced salesman, a slick, disingenuous, slow smile. He put the laptop aside.

"Well, if it ain't Philadelphia. Long time no see, Philadelphia."

"How you doin' Bernier? Brought you somebody. This is Sid. He's lookin' to help out with all the shit you need done around here. You could use some help."

"Well. Hell, yeah. How are you, Sid?"

"Fine," said Sid.

"Where you from?"

"Loonberg. New Hampshire."

"Okay, well. Rodney. Put Sid on the wall with Pietro. You work hard, Sid, you can go far here. Hard work and a good attitude. All you need. Now, Philly. We got business to talk."

"Yes, we do," said Phil. The black coat, Rodney, motioned for Sid to follow and they left the bedroom office of Bernier and his redhead lady friend, took the elevator down, back out of the house and then a long walk across fields behind the barn to more outhouses, including a relatively small chalet perched on the edge of the woods, with trails leading across the fields and down the mountainside.

On the back side of the chalet, built in the Swiss style with a steep metal roof and ornate wooden eaves, Sid saw a pile of field stones and an old long-bed truck with a crane in the bed idling beside the pile. In the driver's seat of the truck, a long-haired, middle-aged guy sat puffing a cigarette. He opened the door when he saw Rodney and Sid come around the corner of the chalet, followed by Rover. He hopped down from the cab. He was rangy, with the slow spring of someone used to physical labor, saving his energy.

"Hey, Pietro," said Rodney. "Got you a helper."

"A helper?" said the man, spitting disgustedly. "Who says I need a fucking helper?"

"Bernier says so," said Rodney.

Pietro sized Sid up wordlessly, staring at him while he finished his cigarette.

"You, ah, familiar with masonry? Stonework?" He threw away the butt.

"No," said Sid.

"Is this your dog?" Rover came over, sniffing around after the tossed cigarette butt.

"Yeah. That's Rover."

"Rover. Of the, ah, thousand seas, eh?"

"Exactly," said Sid.

Rodney was on the phone with his back to them. When he turned around, he put his hands back in his pockets.

"I'll leave you to it," he said disgustedly, glancing curtly up at

them both before stalking away.

III - The Progress of Things

Pietro got his green card in 2007 after he'd served with the Army as an intelligence officer in Iraq. He knew Arabic and stonework from his family background. His father and uncles, Tunisians, had been masons back in Sicily. He chain-smoked Marlboro Reds. He kept cartons of them on the top shelf of a closet in his bedroom in the chalet. Sid and Rover slept at the back of the media room upstairs in a kind of loft space. Sid had a field cot, a stretcher with an aluminum frame, and a rug, a sheepskin to pull over himself and Rover beside him on the floor, the varnished, new floor of wide, antique pine boards. The heat from the woodstove rose into the loft. It was the warmest spot in the chalet. The flatscreen was not plugged into any cable, so it didn't get any channels. There were books in a small bookcase, some volumes of poetry and paperback novels that looked well-thumbed. Bernier's girlfriend, the redhead, was a writer, according to Pietro. Sid imagined the books were hers, things she'd recently read in her college courses, books by Italo Calvino and Alice Walker. She looked well-heeled as did Bernier, educated at private colleges with degrees in business or women's studies or something equally useless. And then Bernier had talked his way into money of one sort or another. The chalet was supposed to be a guesthouse for friends of Bernier's. Pietro was sleeping in the unfurnished bedroom, just a cot like Sids. They worked on the stone wall that was supposed to enclose five acres of sheep pasture. The sheep were going to be trucked in from out West, a special breed of Spanish sheep, along with some border collies, said Pietro. The girlfriend was behind most of the projects on the property, and she would come by with Bernier every so often, said Pietro, to check on the progress of things. She would chat with you, while Bernier was normally antisocial. The chalet had been completed in the summer, and now they were supposed to do the wall. The recently cleared, plowed, and seeded field would be ready for the sheep in the spring, and then the guests would come out to the guesthouse starting next summer. But that was all the way off in the future. Bernier had other plans that had nothing to do with sheep. That was another story. But in the meantime, they worked with the truck and the crane and the piles of field stones scattered along the future trajectory of the field wall. Sid was pretty handy, as it turned out. He lined up stakes and strung a level for the crane to work off, and he could choose by the shape of the stones, lay them in place with certainty, no trembling nor doubt, a stable, solid structure that would stand despite gravity and decay.

At night, Pietro cooked their food. It turned out that he liked to talk while he smoked cigarettes after dinner. He asked Sid about jail, and Sid tried to answer as truthfully as he could. There wasn't a lot to say. Pietro puffed and nodded. Pietro told him about the towns in southern Iraq along the Tigris where he'd served with a detachment of Rangers. The people there had treated them with trepidation and never shrinking distance, but Pietro knew why. He understood their allegiance to their houses, their domestic animals, the patchwork of fields and scattered days of rain in the winter months like a sprinkling of water on their parched tongues. They were essential people, allied still to the natural world, whose vision was scaffolded to seasons and the memory of seasons. The soldiers in Pietro's squad had seemed to exist in a vacuum between their videogaming youth and their decrepit old age, a romantic period that was up to them to embellish with the trinkets and souvenirs of that exotic war of opportunity. They were pitted in Iraq, because of the politics and the circumstances, against the very idea of survival, against the mother planet. Pietro had survived his time in the US Army, just like Sid had survived his time in the correctional facility. And so they had that in common. Neither of them had much to say after it was clear that their mutual survival also reflected their common disability. They shared an understanding that every blow struck was a clue to the lines of God's will, that every heart was a knot, and only death was a universal solvent that erased the savor of sweat and tears.

They worked in the rain and snow of late fall and early winter. Sid would warm his hands, taking off the gloves and bending his knees over them, sandwiching them in his large calves and thighs while Pietro backed the crane off to lift the larger stones. Sid supplemented their working piles by wheelbarrowing over mountains of rubble stones that would be the heart used to secure the larger field stones and fill in gaps in the courses.

Long days and nights passed. It was mid-winter. Groceries were laid in the doorway of the chalet, boxes of provisions meant to last a month at a time. Rover's coat filled out on leftovers of cheap flank steaks and factory-farmed eggs. Sid was feeling less pain, thinking about his feet less, in any case. Pietro promised he would locate a new pair of boots and some socks for him. They liked to watch Rover run, bounding through snow drifts in the woods that were part of Belknap Mountain State Forest. Rover could run forever. It made Sid feel good to watch. Sometimes Sid spotted Rodney or the Asian kid driving the Lexus 4x4 with boxes loaded in the back seat, but they either were out in the field working, moving imperceptibly along the edge of the wide, tall, curling wall of stone, a barrier against predators and premature ends, or he was coming back through the woods like one of his Beothuk, pausing in the trees to see what was out in the world of the race of men.

They were stuck inside at Christmas time. They weren't sure what day it was, but Pietro thought it was the twenty-fourth, Christmas Eve, when all was supposed to be silent and peaceful. In the correctional facility, it had been a time, usually, of heightened alertness, as some of the inmates invariably became surly, and arguments would start over opened packages, stolen goods, and insults of one kind or another that made a mockery of the season.

A snowstorm blanked out the windows. There had been four bottles of whiskey in the last box. They were well into the third bottle. Pietro also had a treasure, a shoebox full of hash, and an old fashioned hash pipe made of olive wood. He and Sid were getting anxious and paranoid with the snow and the lack of air and contact with fellow humans. Sid's feet hurt like hell, and he wished sometimes for pain medication that would blank out the time. He tried to explain what it was like to be in such pain. Pietro understood. For him, hash and whiskey and long days of hard physical work did the trick of killing the sorrows he felt. It was exchanging one kind of chain for another, he realized, but it was a fair and equitable compromise, and he felt like he could honestly recommend it as a course of action.

Pietro opened a window. Sid suggested they hike into Meredith and see a movie. Pietro was agreeable to the plan. There was a lot of snow, but the road into Gilmanton wasn't too far down the mountain, Sid said. If they left now, they could make it to the road before dark and hitch a ride with one of the town's plough trucks, said Sid. Those guys wouldn't ask questions. They could say their truck had broken down. They could say that it was no big deal, they just needed a part. They worked out the details of what to do in Meredith besides seeing a movie. They would go to a bar, meet some tourists. Then they heard a truck's rumbling engine, somebody driving up to the chalet.

"Open the door, Sid. See who it is there," said Pietro.

Rover barked. He would not stop.

Sid opened the door. The wind blew sideways flakes of snow up into his face, and he shielded his eyes to see.

"Yo. Sid Green."

Phil Collins stood in the door as the storm whipped around him.

"You bigger than the mountain, Sid."

"Come on in and get out of the snow, Philadelphia," said Sid.

"And look at the fuckin' dog, would you?" said Phil.

"Have a whiskey, Phil," said Sid.

"Well, don't mind if I do. They takin' care of you boys," said Phil, stamping his boots and loosening his coat.

Pietro poured a new glass from the counter and refilled the two on the table. Phil took the glass that Pietro extended.

"Cheers," said Pietro, sagely waiting for the two others to lift theirs.

Phil drank some of the whiskey and swallowed.

"Well, I got some news for you, bruh. We got some business to do and it's goin' down tonight." He paused for dramatic effect, studying the whiskey in the juice glass in the light of the kitchen's sole bulb.

"What are you talking about?" said Pietro.

"Strictly a need to know. Now Sid, I know you know how to handle a snowmobile 'cause you a woodman. Ain't that right?" said Phil.

"Yeah. Used to have one of them Skidoos," said Sid. "Ran around a little in the old days."

"Good, you're gonna drive like a bat outta hell tonight. And you, my man," Phil pointed at Pietro. "You comin along, too. All hands on deck. That's the word from Bernier."

"Is he here?" asked Pietro.

"He is indeed here," said Phil.

Later that night, it was still snowing. Sid talked to Rover, trying to tell him he'd be back soon. He shut the door of the chalet with the dog inside, and he and Pietro set out to the main house, trudging across the hill with one headlamp between them on Sid's forehead, strapped over the tight wool cap that Pietro had located for him. He pulled the zipped front of his canvas coat tighter around him as he walked and wished he had a better outfit underneath than the Jack Daniels hoodie. The fronts to the prison-issued boots were starting to wear thin, and the soles felt like they were flapping. It must have been close to ten degrees and falling to near zero by dawn, the radio in the truck said. The next day, Christmas, was supposed to warm up to near fifteen to thirty north to south, it said. The doors to the barn were open. Overhead lights hanging from the ceiling revealed a knot of blank-faced men hanging around two trucks pulled back to the doors with low-bed trailers attached. The trailers inside the barn under the floodlights carried two snowmobiles apiece. The people around the barn floor looked up as the truck doors slammed. Sid and Pietro got out and walked swiftly inside to shelter.

Bernier and his girlfriend were dressed in matching quilted coats and insulated hunting boots. Bernier had a Patriots ball cap on that looked like he'd slept with it under his pillow recently to give it an authentic, worn look. And the girlfriend wore a Santa hat up top of her head, going for a down home, pep rally appeal. There were one piece, padded, zero degree suits in cardboard boxes, brand new suits for Pietro and Sid and a few of the other guys, brown, sullen, sunken faces on them, to put on. Phil explained they would ride in the trucks and then get on the snowmobiles for a trek across the lake. The trucks would wait on the road. Out on the lake they would be met by an airplane that would come in and land on the snow. Someone passed around red plastic cups of eggnog spiked with whiskey to cheer them up, to no avail. Bernier's girlfriend laughed loudly at something Bernier said. Nobody else laughed. Sid tried to get close once he had pulled on his suit, which was a little tight. Bernier noticed him on the outskirts of the little knot of men surrounding him and his girlfriend in the truck cab.

"How's that fit? You okay?" asked Bernier.

"Yeah, it's fine. Could use some gloves, though, if I'm driving," said Sid, lifting his large bare hands, staring past Bernier.

"Gloves, right. That makes sense. Let's see. Rodney. Any gloves? Where are the gloves? Thought we ordered gloves."

"Yeah, we got some gloves. Duncan, where are the gloves?"

The Asian kid, Duncan, was sent out to make the short walk to the mansion to get the boxes of gloves they'd forgotten there. When he came back, his arms were full of boxes with a thick layer of snow all over them. Duncan bravely walked back to them as the men parted to make a path for him. He dropped the boxes on the ground behind the truck as some of the men shifted themselves around uncomfortably in the new insulated suits. Sid straightened from where he was leaning against the wall of the barn, looking pointedly uninterested in the proceedings. He went over to where the girlfriend was handing out gloves. It reminded him of high school somehow. He looked the girlfriend in the eyes, trying to communicate his disdain for the books by Alice Walker and Italo Calvino, nothing against any of them personally, just the collected banality of books in the future guesthouse for eco-tourists.

But the girlfriend smiled and looked past him. Bernier stood in the bed of the truck and gallantly gave a speech about teamwork and triumph against the wicked that denied victory except if taken by the toughest, the quickest, the bravest, most daring. Bernier was a prophet of venality, and his team were a bunch of anonymous, faceless, faithless dead-enders held together by the thin hopes of an easy payday, Phil included. Sid saw the way Phil's mouth tightened as Bernier gave off his litany in a smile that rubbed the grain of his facial musculature.

The trucks started. Sid and Pietro sat in the second row of the first truck. They started out down the mountain road through wind-driven banks of snow. The trucks followed each other down the road and out along the state highway. At the intersection with Route 21 they took slow left turns through a foot or two of snow. At the end of the road, they dead-stopped. In the light of the headlights they lowered the gate on the trailer of the first truck. Sid and another guy pulled on their gloves and started the snowmobiles and backed them down off the trailers. Then four snowmobiles started out in a line onto the frozen, snow-covered surface of the lake. There was no visibility other than the headlights of the snowmobiles. The night sky and the lake surface were indistinguishable. Pietro sat behind Sid. The cold rushed past them, barely perceptible, except around their faces that quickly became numb. Then in the sky a light appeared in a blue halo and circled the storm above them. The snowmobiles stopped, beams of light shooting across the lake through the snowfall, and the men watched as the plane lowered itself to the surface of the lake and came to a glide in darkness, shutting off its wing and tail lights. The line of snowmobiles revved engines again and swiftly scuttled across the snow-covered ice, approaching the airplane.

From the back of the plane, barely visible, men shouted something at them, throwing large parcels out an open flap onto the snow. Men in the snowmobiles jumped off the backs and began slowly to collect the parcels off the snow and stack them on tarps they unfolded and held down behind the airplane in the snow and wind. The whole operation took about an hour. The plastic-wrapped packages were folded up in the tarps. The tarps were tied off the back of the snowmobiles with parachute cord. Then they pulled like sleds back to the landing across the lake. They loaded the packages into the cabs of the two trucks. They pulled the tarps over the cabs and tied them down while the drivers, Sid among them, got the snowmobiles back onto their trailers. The men shouted. Sid turned and saw the lights on the airplane lift off the lake and take a slow ascent and quickly disappear, swallowed by the storm once again.

Most of the men were too cold and their faces too numb to make words come out. One by one, they scrambled back in the trucks. They wouldn't look at one another, sunk in private miseries, willing the time to go by as fast as possible until they could thaw out in some warm shelter. The trucks started up and slowly ground through the unplowed road back up the mountain, crossing no traffic in the silent night.

Back in the barn, Bernier and his girlfriend waited: dancing, playing music, the forest soundscapes from wireless speakers. As the men disembarked, they handed out red plastic cups of hot spiked eggnog and greeted the men with thanks and smiles. Some of the men talked to one another in a language Sid didn't recognize.

"Where are these guys from?" he asked Pietro.

"Bhutan. Refugees," said Pietro. "Some they pull from the shelter in Nashua. Bernier knows the people that run it. Some church group."

"What?"

"Yeah, Bernier. Some non-profit. They both. Him and Carissa. Help the homeless or something," said Pietro.

"I guess we're not going into Meredith," said Sid.

"No, not tonight," said Pietro.

Sid's hands and feet were numb. There was a barrel with a fire going. He warmed his hands over the fire. Phil was there.

"Yo, Sid," said Phil. "Check this out." He handed Sid a stone, perfectly round, weathered and worn to a smooth finish.

"What is it?" asked Sid.

"Found it in the snow in the lake," said Phil. "I thought of you. Merry Christmas." Phil laughed.

"Well, thanks," said Sid, flipping the stone.

"Any word from Ruth?" he asked.

"Nah," said Phil. "Forget that bitch. Imma see you later, Sid. You take care."

"See ya, Philadelphia," said Sid. Philadelphia drove out in the early morning hours from the party in the barn, leaving in his old Ram truck with a load of snow in the cab. It seemed to be running well enough. Pietro and Sid headed back to the chalet. Rover greeted them with bounds and hungry, smacking sounds. Pietro started the fire back in the wood stove, blowing on the hot embers underneath the fresh log. Sid poured out some food into Rover's bowl and changed his water. Then he and the dog climbed up to the media room, and Sid pulled off his wet clothes and pulled the sheepskin rug over himself in the cot, clutching the stone Phil had given him still in his left hand. The dog curled up underneath the cot. The snow slid suddenly off the roof and landed on the ground with a thud.

The days of waiting went on. Time stretched endlessly out into the sky and deep within, to the place where it lies coiled like a sea serpent, until the day we die and we rejoin the timeless koa, the heroes who ride beyond the wave. The men of the Karawa looked out to sea, to the crown of the ocean for a sign. They turned to me, a child, the daughter of the departed chief, and I alone could know the path across the water to better lands. We were looking for a pleasant bay to settle. The outriggers were ready, but I waited. You came to me, brother.

'The sea turtles are abandoning us. It is time,' you said.

It was true the turtles and their sisters the birds had disappeared together one morning to the east, silently, embarrassed at our stubbornness and lack of hearing. They thought the gods must have abandoned us to the coming storm, to the onslaught of the evil ones that had been foretold by the mothers of the living over the fires of many nights past.

I looked to you, for you were my brother, but it was not time.

'How do you know?' you asked me.

'That's not for you to inquire,' I said. 'I am the daughter, the chosen one. Fortune has placed the wreath of flowers on my head.'

'But what signs are you pursuing? What tracks have you followed over the waves to the shoals of mahi mahi and bonito?'

'These are tracks that are only visible to the blind. I have plucked my eyes out, brother, for the good of the Karawa,' I said.

You turned away and began to trace patterns in the sand with your big toe.

You came to me the next morning when the sun had split open the sky with its treasure, scattering the beacons of the stars for another day.

'Haoli. The wind has abandoned us.'

It was true. Our mother wind had seemed to fall asleep. We were forgetting who we even were or where even we had come from. The memories of Rairatea were growing dim among the warriors and the mothers walked the strip of sand in circles, leaving their babies behind. The leaves of the palm tree hung like tears and the sky seemed like it would burst with a secret longing.

'Trust me,' I said to you and you looked at me angrily then and stomped away, dashing into the water and throwing off spumes from your hot back as you swam over the reef.

The next day I was looking out over the water, hoping to hear the voices of our ancestors calling, when you came to me.

'The dolphin have also left, and you still have nothing. What can I tell the people?'

'Trust me. They must wait until the signs are there. I will know when and where to set the prows of the outriggers.'

'But the babies are crying out and the mothers' breasts are running dry.'

'We can make food from the stores of breadfruit buried in the hole of Molekoni.'

The breadfruit was bitter but it kept us alive for many more weeks. The sea turned clear and white even with no wind. The people were lazy, falling around on the sand, shorn of purpose or thought of any kind. The mothers forgot the names of their children.

It was the night of the new moon. I prayed to the star of the North, the star that never wavered as we circled. You slept beside me, trusting and loving Moki. The next morning, I knew that it was your heart that the gods had answered. The sea began to grow as the wind developed from the North. The leaves of the palms awakened and the mothers cried out for their children, using their holy names.

You came to me with breadfruit, but I told you to eat. It was the last of the stores from the hole of Molekoni.

'Tell the men of the Karawa to prepare the outriggers. We will launch today and sail with the new wind.'

'But we have never sailed with this wind,' you said.

'Look at the sea. It is a good, joyous sea. It is truly for us that this wind blows, Moki.'

It was the first time ever that I had truly seen you smile.

We launched the boats and sailed into the southern sea as the ocean's crown rose behind us. The waves slapped under the keels. The warriors pulled the long paddles, and the mothers sang to their children. Soon we could see the dolphins, the sea turtles, and their siblings the birds.

But you, Moki. You never smiled again even when we reached the new shores and set upright the waiting moai on the flanks of the island.

Bernier and his girlfriend stayed on in the mansion. They went skiing at Gunstock and came back with friends. Sid watched the comings and goings from around the corner of the chalet. He wanted to get off that mountain. He missed Ruth and Leesha and wanted to talk to Ruth, see how she was. Ruth Rendell. He borrowed Pietro's phone and did a search for her name. No numbers came up. Then he remembered the name of the store where Ruth worked. The Pacha Mama. He and Pietro were out laying stones in sub-freezing weather, using insulated gloves and keeping a couple of thermoses full of steaming coffee in the cab of the truck. They dug down to the ground with picks and shovels and scratched out a flat pad for the foundation stones. They couldn't set stakes because they wouldn't go into the frozen ground, so they had to line up the wall by eye. Pietro kept meaning to ask Bernier for a laser level, but they were doing well enough just lining up the progress of it as they went. That night, Sid asked Pietro if he could use the phone again the next day to call the store in Concord. Pietro agreed. But the next morning, Rodney showed up early and ordered them up to the mansion in fifteen minutes.

It was clear to Sid that he needed to get out, that his days of indentured servitude needed to be behind him. Pietro wanted them to leave together once the weather improved and the wall was finished. But Sid couldn't wait any longer. It was true that the time went by quickly. But he couldn't help dreaming of city streets, women entering and exiting doors, faces, smells, a dizzying torrent of life that swept so quickly into the future that it blinded you before you could realize it. Rover circled his spot by the woodstove and lay down. Sid closed the door and turned towards the mansion. Pietro was already halfway up the hill, crunching through the remnants of snow.

The two utility vans went from the barn. One was blue and the other was white. Rodney and Duncan drove. Sid and Pietro were passengers with Duncan's van. Phil and another Bhutanese guy named Suraj went with Rodney. The highway was packed going north, in the other direction, a line of traffic patiently coming at them, Subarus and Mini Coopers with skiing equipment on the roof racks. Sid watched the turquoise roof of L.L. Bean and the gold dome of the capitol building slide by. They drove down the west side of Manchester on 203, snaking expertly in and out of traffic and through the tolls with the EZ Pass. Sid had never been through the EZ Pass before. That was a new thing, an improvement. It made little difference to Sid. It just meant there was no fleeting human face to take their money and register a quick moment of shared, withered humanity through the tolls. In Nashua they got off on Amherst Street and headed west, pulling a U-turn a couple of blocks past the exit. Then they turned into a little strip mall with an outlet selling craft brew supplies, a nail salon, a sandwich shop, and a car parts place. They parked in the back of the strip mall, facing a loading dock across the lot, both vans with the engines running. Duncan was on the phone with someone. Sid could see Rodney through the window of his passenger side. Rodney was on the phone also.

They waited in the parking lot for a good half hour before someone appeared on the loading dock. A short man in dark clothes, he motioned vaguely with his hand and seemed to be looking at them. Duncan put the van in gear and began to roll across the lot, checking in the direction of Amherst Street for traffic.

"Fuck," said Duncan. Sid looked the way of Amherst Street. Two police cars had pulled up and stopped, blocking that exit.

"Gun it," said Sid. Duncan did what he said, screeching tires to get around to the parking lot's opposite access. The police cars sounded their sirens. Two more swung into the lot ahead of them. Rodney's van with Phil and Suraj crashed into a wall in an attempt to swerve past the cruisers. Duncan slammed the brakes. Pietro reached down and grabbed a couple of baggies, stuffing them in his coat.

"See you, mates," he yelled. Jettisoning out the door of the van, he ran helter skelter across the lot. Sid watched as two policemen chased Pietro down and tackled him. Duncan was out in the lot with his hands up. Sid did the same as Pietro, grabbed some baggies behind the seat on the floor of the van and stuffed them down his pants. Exiting on the opposite side, he dashed across the lot and vaulted onto the loading dock, ducked under a screen of plastic and into what was the back room of the craft brewery. The snap of gunfire sounded behind him.

Sid barrelled through the craft brewery, knocking over racks of empty carboys and sample distillery kits. As he went out the front door, one store clerk said to another:

"There he goes. Gonna be one of those days."

"Get down!" warned the other. The clerks dove to the floor as two policemen came running in from the back after the fleeing figure of Sid, who was on his way, knees pumping like the old days down the middle of Amherst Street, bringing traffic to a screeching halt in both directions.

At the Dunkin Donuts, a car was waiting to enter traffic in the drive-thru exit. Sid hauled open the side door of the Impala and jumped in. The man who was driving looked at Sid squint-eyed as he clambered in and lowered under the dash.

"I'm looking for a ride. Sorry," said Sid.

"I don't take no freeloaders. You payin'?"

"Of course. Just get going."

"What's your big hurry?"

"I'm late," said Sid. "I'll pay you."

Sid stretched and quickly pulled two bills from his front pocket. He was down to forty dollars from the correctional facility gate money. As they drove down the avenue towards the west in the slow moving traffic, Sid held out the twenty-dollar bill. The man looked at it and took it from his fingers. Sirens sounded in the background.

"I guess that makes it real," said Sid.

"What's real?" said the driver.

"Everything has a price," said Sid. The driver mumbled something he couldn't catch. Sid didn't ask for names. That would have been crazy.

The days were still short. It was mid-morning with a low sun behind low clouds. Sid was in Milford, walking in a part of town where the front windows had no curtains and no lightbulbs in the sockets above the doors. A woman sat in a chair in a curtainless window in a recently re-sided home with a neatly laid brick foundation and several empty spaces in a small parking lot in the front yard. Sid walked up and knocked on the door.

"Excuse me. Is there a room available here?" he asked.

"You'd have ta see Valerie," said the woman. She had a soft voice, but harsh lines around the mouth, and with bangs of peroxide-damaged hair above her eyes. She was almost as big as Sid.

"Is Valerie the…?

"She manages the property. You lookin' ta stay sober?"

"Yeah."

"It's 300 bucks a week. How you goin' ta pay for that?"

"I have no idea. I don't have 300 bucks."

"Well, you can apply for the temporary aid deal. But you have ta be approved by the residents."

"Okay."

"Is that what you really want?"

"I don't know what I really want."

"Well, sit down inside here and think about it. Valerie will be here soon. What's your name?"

"Sid."

"Sid. Sit down and think about what you really want. If you're ready for this step."

"Okay, what's your name?"

"My name? Izzie."

"Okay. Izzie. What I really want is to get my dog."

"Where is he?"

"Somewhere up North. Around the Laconia area."

"How you gonna do that? You need ta get sober ta take care of a dog, right?"

"Uhm." Sid wondered how he was ever going to get back to Bernier's chalet to collect Rover. He wondered whether at some point the weight of jettisoned lives would be enough to cause him to lie down and never get back up.

"Sounds to me like you need ta sit down and wait for Valerie. She'll walk ya through the forms. Come on."

Izzie showed him to a side chair in the living room. The television was on. Kelly Clarkson did a cover of a One Direction hit song. Someone showed how to grill a steak. Kelly interviewed Rob Gronkowski. After that, Sid lost interest in the television and noticed Izzie was knitting something. She was about twenty-eight or so, he guessed, too young to have taken up knitting. Still, it was the kind of thing that may have recently been featured on a television segment which he would have missed since television in jail was restricted to only a few cells for well-connected prisoners or the common room pod which rarely worked. Ruth had had no television and the cable in the chalet on Bernier's property had not been fully hooked-up yet. Sid thought about the term hooked-up and how it had started to mean something different than it had before he was in the correctional facility. Sid looked over at Izzie again and stood up. He stretched and asked to use the bathroom. When he came back from the bathroom it was News 9 at Noon. Izzie was gone from the sitting room. There were some magazines and brochures about the Sober Houses program and the non-profit foundation that ran them, Oxford Health. Sid leafed through the brochure, skimming the article. He saw a small box with names of the board of directors and staff of

Oxford Health, and he sat up when he saw John Charles Bernier, who was listed as Chief Operations Officer of a company called Licht, Brown and Associates, with an address in Boston. Sid continued reading down the names of the other board members, and there, he also glommed on to Darrell E. Green of Shuman Brothers at 210 Commonwealth Avenue. That was his brother Darrell. He was sure of it because Darrell's middle name was Elsworth.

"What the fuck?" he said under his breath. He stood up and stuffed the brochure in his coat pocket. It was getting crowded in his pockets with the two bags of heroin inside the coat and now the brochure.

"You want some soup, Sid?'

"Sure," said Sid. It smelled good. Izzie placed a bowl on the epoxy coffee table for him. It had bits of leafy green floating along with cubes of something white.

"It's tofu," said Izzie. "I'm on a diet."

"No, it's good," said Sid. Izzie looked up at him and smiled warily.

Sid finished the soup.

"What time do the others usually show up?" he asked. He was getting antsy. He didn't know what he was going to do. However, he was feeling extremely anxious at the prospect of filling out forms and having to meet Valerie the property manager and the other residents of the sober house. The fact of having just hours earlier escaped police arrest was giving him no pleasure.

“Ryan usually shows up about now after his group therapy. Josephine and Pragya come in at 3:30. They work part-time. June comes in after work.”

“Where does June work?”

“He works for himself. He’s a coder.”

“Is that everyone?”

“That’s it. That’s everybody. We just lost Marden.”

“What happened to Marden?’

“He died. He disappeared a couple of weeks ago. Didn’t make it.”

“That’s too bad.”

“Where’s all this bad shit out there on the street coming from? Don’t it seem like somebody’s trying ta get rid of all of the good people?”

“Yeah. I know.”

“I know it’s hard for you, Sid. How long has it been?”

“Since what?”

“Since ya’ve been clean?”

“A couple of days.”

“Want some more soup?”

“No, listen, I’ve made up my mind. I’m not ready for this. Thanks, anyway. You’ve been very nice. I love the soup.”

“Hey. This isn’t for everyone. I understand.”

“I just need to get going. Find my dog, you know.”

“Yeah. What’re ya gonna do?

“I don’t know. I’ll figure something out. It’s all right.”

"Why dontcha get an Uber?"

"To Laconia?"

"No. Ta the bus station."

"I don't want to go back to Nashua. I think I'll just head up to Manchester. Start hitching."

"Nobody's gonna pick ya up hitching. Ya look like a fucking junkie."

"Well. maybe. Thanks anyway."

"Look, I'll getcha an Uber. I can pay for it."

"Are you serious?"

"Yeah. I mean it. Where do ya wanna go?"

"Anywhere. Manchester's good."

"The mall?"

"Yeah, Why not? Here. I've got this."

Sid stood and produced the two bags of heroin, laying them on the coffee table with a neat slap. Cloth bags wrapped in clear plastic stamped with small printed crossed swords, Arabic lettering and the number 555 inside a red triangle.

"Oh my Gawd."

"Beautiful thing, right? I knew you'd like this, Izzie." Sid felt evil and brilliant, a mastermind, if only for a few seconds, able to provide magic relief and entertainment at will. What a guy, was Sid. This was better than hooking up, better than sex. The only problem was it always hurt worse afterwards, like a wound in a heart that just bled faster. For a few brief moments though, it was a heat that burned a liquid heaven.

Izzie used a paring knife she brought back to the sitting room to slice open a corner of one bag. She boiled up a spoon of the powder.

"I can't believe this shit," she said, extracting the test strip from the spoon. Sid filled up the syringe.

"Yeah," he said.

"Ya got another needle?" asked Izzie, after shooting up a vein in her leg.

"No," said Sid. He burned a batch of it on some tin foil she gave him, and he huffed on the smoke.

The road beneath his feet lifted him with a gentleness that made him a beautiful man. And Izzie and him, everyone was united in the same noble cause. All thoughts of Rover and Leesha and Ruth and his brother Darrell were imbued with a sense of peace, with his past, present, and future conjoined in some rising spiral of pleasure that went into the sky and deep down into every cell of his being.

All he wanted to do was sleep and join the dream forever. He'd left the one bag with Izzie. That left him one entire bag in his coat pocket and twenty dollars. The taxi dropped him at the parking lot of the Manchester mall, and Sid walked inside like a conquering king and sat inside in an empty food court, thanking Izzie in a prayer.

The mall was a wreck, devoid of serious customers or even windowshoppers. The stores were mostly boarded up, just seasonal holdovers selling Christmas decorations or cheap plastic toys. Sid had never been attracted by the prospect of shopping. He was simple in terms of taste and always found himself put off by the garish displays of opulence that constantly were designed to make people like him feel inferior in his growing up years. That was Steve's influence. Steve had always believed in a pure, undiscovered, primal way of life. That had never been enough for Sid, though, as an explanation by which to approach life. It seemed cold and untruthful to the way he felt, which was that everyone, the garish and the beautiful, the opulent and the plain, were united in a journey away from pain, and the best art captured the pain of the journey and made it comprehensible and meaningful for any sort of people. He actually found the empty mall evocative of some past vanity that was pure in its ruined decadence, and he wandered slowly as if in a museum until late at night, awash in a glorious wave. Or maybe he just imagined he'd done all that. Because when the security guard pushed on his shoulder he found himself sitting at a table back in the food court. Popeye Chicken and Taco Beyondo were closing down, and that was it. A strange and menacing table of teenage boys near the Taco Beyondo counter stared at him and laughed.

"Time to go, pal," said the rumpled, overweight security guard. The teenagers laughed. They didn't look like they were having fun, though. Sid stared around in disbelief at being awakened from his dream.

He stepped cautiously back outside, leaving the playland of reflective mirrors behind. He was still rushing, but the cold soon wore any euphoria out of him. Still, he wasn't scared. He caught a ride on the highway going north after standing with his thumb out for a couple of hours, yelling into the darkness as the headlights flared past.

The driver of the Kia Soul wanted to talk. It was his girlfriend's car. He had stolen it from her mother's driveway. His name was Nelson. He had long dirty nails, disgusting even for Sid. He was high as a kite.

"Man, I know you got money. Let's stop and get some food," said Nelson, mystically sensing that Sid was higher than he.

"No, I just want to keep moving down the road, man. You can drop me wherever you can," said Sid, once they were past the tolls. It would be better to step out and keep hitching rather than get stuck with Nelson and his sad story. But it was too late. Nelson craved something, just like him. He would have to acknowledge it. Nelson looked over at him in the light of the dashboard. His eyes, deeply pocketed, were empty of light, black holes.

"What's the worst thing you've ever done?" asked Nelson.

"I don't know. I don't remember," said Sid, looking away.

"You do fucking remember, man. I know you do."

"Hell, I don't. Can't remember," insisted Sid.

"Okay. Well here goes. I, you won't believe this. I like to finger the baby girl."

"I don't care, man," said Sid.

"No, you need to hear this. You ride with me, you listen to my story." Nelson was angry, his voice stringy and squawky like a chicken.

"I'd rather get out. Let me out," said Sid insistently.

Nelson stepped on the gas to get around a tractor trailer. It was drizzling, freezing rain. He had the heat going strong in the Kia Soul. The radio was playing *Iris* by the Goo Goo Dolls.

"*When everything's meant to be broken,*

I just want you to know who I am…"

"My girlfriend's baby girl, man. Nothing better to me, man." Nelson laughed. Or was it a cry.

Sid didn't actually decide anything. But his hand flashed over and grabbed Nelson around the neck, pushing his head up and back against the headrest with a force that instantly snapped the cartilage between his third and fourth vertebra. The Soul careened into a guardrail, hit and spun headlong into the rapidly slowing tractor trailer, bounced and spun, and came to a stop in the median between the northbound and southbound lanes. The airbags had exploded. They released their pressurized air with a hiss. Sid looked up and saw the shattered windshield through the dust of the receding air bags, the sleet coming through the glass, the crumpled front of the vehicle, and the limp body of Nelson slumped against the door of the car. He studied Nelson's face in the light of the city of Concord reflecting off the low clouds. He looked better now, more at peace.

He hopped out and ran across the empty northbound highway. The tractor trailer driver was coming back down the highway on foot after parking the truck in the breakdown lane. He didn't see Sid jump the guardrail and hustle down the embankment, through the underbrush until he reached the road that paralleled the river and began to walk.

The houses were dark. The people were sleeping. Frozen sleet covered Sid head to toe, and eventually everything on him was soaking wet. He felt like taking off his shoes, but thought he'd keep walking until they just fell off. His feet had no feeling in them. The only thing he could think of was food and coffee, which he associated with better times. The food could be pancakes and sausages or it could be bacon and scrambled eggs. Sid liked either fantasy. The sun lightened the sky to a dull grey while the ice storm turned to a steady, wet drizzle. The houses came closer together. He stood on the road under the highway, past a couple of gas stations. There were people from well-heated houses filling up their perfectly maintained cars and throwing down some pleasantly hot muffins on the go. The skin that held it all together was exceedingly thin, thought Sid. The life of the country was more like a sheen of gasoline on troubled waters, capable of either lighting in a quick rush of accelerated energy or dissipating away, washed out by the blows nature would throw at them. Fire or water, that was the only choice on offer, it seemed.

Sid waited around the corner in the entrance to the YMCA. He sat shivering on the curb. When he sensed traffic had picked up to a decent pitch of mid-morning activity, he stood. He tried to arrange the hair on his head with his numbed, pickled fingers and checked his reflection in the side mirror of one of the parked cars on the street, leaning down and sticking his face near the car. He was older than he'd once been. Luckily, Ruth recognized him immediately and came around from behind the counter. She led him by the elbow out the door onto the street. It was still drizzling. They stood in the door and Ruth stared up at him, unable to think of words.

"What happened to you?" asked Sid.

"I came. You weren't there. Only the old lady. She said she didn't know where you were."

"I, uh, had a job," mumbled Sid.

"That's okay, Sid. I missed you. Leesha too. Why didn't you call?"

"I never had a phone."

"You could have borrowed one."

"I couldn't remember your last name."

"Sid. You're all wet."

"I'm hungry, Ruth."

"Where've you been? Never mind."

"My feet are killin' me."

"Okay. Okay," said Ruth.

She went inside and came back out a minute later.

"It's slow. I got a couple of hours off for lunch. Unpaid, but you take what you can get, right?" asked Ruth.

"That's right."

"Come on. I've got Lesli's car."

"Oh, yeah?"

"Yeah, she's in California visiting her family with Boyle. You remember Boyle?'

"The kid living with her?"

"Yeah, that's Leesha's brother."

"What?"

"Yeah, their mom and dad died. Leesha survived the house fire. The firemen just gave her to Boyle when he got home. He was in his senior year."

"What? You never told me that."

"Yeah."

Ruth had decided the time was right to tell him the story about Leesha while they walked the couple of blocks to the parking lot where she kept the car. It was a strange moment. It was just another day in the winter, but Sid felt like bells were ringing. Plough trucks were salting the roads. He was light-headed and felt like he might take flight despite his flat feet and the correctional facility boots that were barely staying on. He tried to stop his chattering teeth so he could hear what Ruth was saying.They walked around inside the parking lot, found Lesli's car, and got in. Ruth started the car while she continued her story.

"So the state says since I got kicked out they want Leesha in the foster care program. So, I'm fightin' that. Lesli's helping with that. But then she has her hands full with Peter. They're actually legally not married, but he's living in his van somewhere in South Carolina. If he comes back I'm lookin' to find my own place, of course. I mean Lesli says I can stay there, but Peter's been an asshole to me in the past."

"What happened to the house on North Main where you were at?"

"Fernaldi raised the rent. Blood sucker. He wants twelve fifty a month now. There's no way I could afford it, Sid."

"What if I got a job?"

"If you got a job and helped out with the rent? Yeah, maybe. But where's Rover?"

"It's a long story."

Ruth drove out of the parking lot.

"I'm going to take you up to the Goodwill, Sid. Buy you some clothes."

Sid relaxed and found his eyes closing with the heat in the car. Ruth parked the car, and Sid opened his eyes. He mumbled something. He wasn't quite awake.

The rain had stopped. Inside the Goodwill, Sid tried on some t-shirts Ruth picked out off the rack for him along with a couple of pants. One of the pants fit him without a belt. He kept on one of the t-shirts, and the pair of pants, and a new hooded sweatshirt that was faded green that said Rehoboth Beach. Then, while Ruth looked at the toys for something for Leesha, Sid pulled on a pair of insulated boots. They were Milwaukee hunting boots, worn, but still relatively fine. They were a little big with no socks, but then, with a new pair of socks, they would fit better than anything he'd worn in years. He bundled his wet clothes, stuck them all inside the worn correctional facility boots. He put the coat back on with the heroin baggie and the folded Oxford Health brochure in the inside pocket. He left the old correctional facility boots just outside the fitting room so one of the attendants would see them. They looked like a picture of his former self, the shedded boots of a wasted life.

“Look at the boots, Ruth.” Sid proudly pulled up the pants leg with the price tag hanging off his waist so she could have a view of the boots on him.

“How much are they?” she asked.

“Sixteen bucks,” said Sid.

“Okay,” said Ruth.

“What’d you get for Leesha?” he asked.

“This here. She loves board games,” said Ruth, holding up a box in one hand. She had her bag over one shoulder, and they were on their way to the cashier.

Sid fell asleep in the car. Ruth parked on Main Street in front of the Holiday Inn. She pushed Sid to wake him up. It was warm in the car. He didn’t want to think about anything else except the new socks and boots on his dry feet. He wished he and Ruth were making love.

“What do you want to do, Sid?”

“Where are we?”

“I’ve got to work in an hour. Why don’t I drive you to Lesli’s house and you can stay there while she’s in California. She’s coming back on Friday, I think.

“What day is it?

“Today is Monday. Where’s Rover?”

“You’ve got to drive me up to Gilford.”

“I don’t have time.”

"Man, I just want to sleep, Ruth. Just take me to Lesli's house, then."

"What? No. You've got to get Rover. Where is he?"

"He's in this house. They'll probably forget he's even there."

"Who will?"

"Bernier will."

Ruth thought for a bit.

"Bernier. Who's he?"

"He's this guy," said Sid.

"Sounds bad."

"Yeah."

"What are you going to do?"

"I don't know. I just want to sleep."

"You can't sleep. You have to get Rover, Sid."

"I'm so tired, Ruth."

"You need to find Rover. What if he dies?"

"Well, buy me some coffee, at least."

"All right."

Ruth pulled a U-turn at the four-way intersection, got back on the highway and drove north. At Tilton she got off and stopped at the McDonalds. Sid used the bathroom while Ruth bought food: two hamburgers, a coffee, and french fries. Sid ate in the car. Ruth talked on the phone with Leesha at the daycare center in Bow. She explained to the woman that she would be late picking her daughter up. The woman wasn't happy about it. Ruth cursed as she got off the phone. She put the phone in the well between the seats.They got on the road and drove towards Gilford. Sid picked out the turnoff for the mountain off Route 26. He told Ruth to pull over on the side of the road and park. He pulled out the bag of heroin from his coat.

"This is what Bernier does," said Sid.

"What is that?"

"Smack."

"Sid. That there's evil shit. Are you kidding?"

"I'm so bent. If I don't get lit right now I'm fucking dead in the water."

"It's going to hurt your ability to have any kind of meaningful relationship with anyone. You going to choose that?"

"Are you serious? Meaningful? What's that shit?"

"Give me that. Where's Rover?"

"At the top of this fucking mountain."

"Well, let's go," Ruth said. She took the bag and put it in the doorwell on her side. Sid sat glumly silent while the car wound its way up the icy, unploughed road, rutted with snow tire treads. When they slowly came out on the rise through the trees, Sid looked up and saw a fleet of cars surrounding the mansion.

'Shit," said Sid. Ruth stopped the car suddenly and pulled on the parking brake. She left the motor running. They sat in silence in the car for a minute before either of them spoke.

"What are you going to do?" asked Ruth.

"Give me the smack," said Sid.

"No."

"Do you know how much money that's worth?"

"I don't care, it's not yours. You give it back wherever you got it."

"You are out of your mind. Give me that fucking bag," Sid leaned over and tried to grab the baggie out of her doorwell. Ruth chopped at his shoulder with both hands, and Sid withdrew.

"Ow," he said.

"Go get Rover."

"I can't do it without gettin' cooked, Ruth. You have no idea what it's like to be a junkie."

"You're not a junkie."

"Well, fuck you then. Wait here. Don't move," said Sid.

He got out of the car unsteadily. He felt like he was about to vomit. His eyes were swelling and about to pop from his skull. The snow crunching under his boots seemed distant and oddly out of sync with his steps. The lay of the hill, as familiar as it had been just a day or so previous, seemed like a distant planet to him now.

He skirted the mansion and went around circuitously, sticking to the edge of fields, lugging himself across the drifts of snow until he reached the chalet. The front door was blocked by three feet of snow blown by the wind. Sid called out Rover's name. He started to dig out with a scraper he found in the cab of the truck. When he moved his head, he got dizzy, but he kept digging. He felt his heart beating -- hard, painful pangs in his chest. If he died, he would die getting Rover out. He heard a bark inside. He dug out enough space to stand and get at the latch. Opening the unlocked door a crack, Sid felt the dog's body push to get through. He fell back into the snowdrift, clutching at Rover. He held him until he'd gotten the complaints and the moaning yowls of grief out of his system. Sid felt like he could stay there forever in the shelter of the space he'd dug out, holding Rover close to him.

The car was still there, with the motor running. Ruth spoke Rover's name in delight when Sid opened the door and got in with the dog. The sun was going down behind them, having popped out at last from the clouds.

"Sid. You found him. Good job."

"LET'S GO! Get out of here!" said Sid. He imagined the doors of the barn opening and swarms of Benier's men coming out to get them. Bernier's mansion was lit like a Christmas tree, with a large gathering going on inside. Ruth turned around, skidding out in the snowy field, tires screeching.

IV - Basket Case

The snow was drifting slowly down, glints of fragmented reality. Already there were a couple of new inches standing up on the rails of the front porch that Sid could see through the window. Behind him, Ruth moved across the living room brushing Leesha's hair and getting her dressed. Lesli was on the road with Peter, her boyfriend. Boyle, Leesha's brother, went out before dawn in his rebuilt Ridgeline. He worked at a supported living facility, Pleasant Vale. The sound of the truck had woken Sid. He hadn't slept since then.

It was Sid's first day at the Market Basket on Storrs Road. Ruth had shepherded him through the application on Friday, and by Saturday afternoon, they'd called to offer him a spot starting Monday morning in the produce department. Sid had lied and said he had experience running a floor buffing machine. It was a part-time job, mornings from 6:00 to 10:30.

Sid dressed and brushed his teeth in the shared bathroom. He was still dizzy when he moved his head. He hadn't eaten a full meal in days, but taking Rover out for walks in the woods again meant he was on the mend. Leesha tugged his arm and wanted to show him something she'd made. He turned around in the half light coming from the kitchen which shone on her face in the hall, the big front teeth as she smiled.

"Sid, I made this for you."

“Aw, thank you, Leesha.”

It was a slice of toast with an animal face made out of peanut butter and banana slices. The banana slices came sliding off and fell silently on the carpet.

“I don’t really deserve this,” said Sid. Leesha turned around to Ruth.

“Of course you do,” said Ruth, from the kitchen.

Rover ate the banana slices. Sid looked at Leesha and smiled. He picked up a slice Rover had left behind and held it in his fingers.

“It’s Sid’s first day,” said Ruth, coming down the hall. She took the plate from Leesha and the slice of banana from Sid’s fingers.

“First day of school?” asked Leesha.

“Yes, first day of school, Leesh. What do you think?” said Sid.

“No, it’s not of school. Don’t lie to her, Sid,” said Ruth.

“Come on, Let’s go. Get in the car, Leesha,” said Ruth. Sid finished the toast. He pulled his coat on. They were going in Lesli’s car. The sun was beginning to put a little light in the sky, showing up the crud-brown snow banks on either side of the stone walls that lined the road. Cars still had their headlights on, driving the backroads. Ruth played her hit list of music off of Spotify. Sid stayed silent, and Leesha fell asleep in the back seat, leaning against the curled up body of Rover. Sid looked in the back of the car at the sleeping figures of Leesha and Rover, once they were going. He didn’t want to think about the morning ahead. It was probably going to be easy, but he felt a dread of it for some unexplained reason, as if it was the one piece of the puzzle that eluded his attempt to build a new life.

“Nice, isn’t it?’ said Ruth, glancing over at him.

“Yes,” said Sid. “It is.”

“When you finish today, walk up to the store. Okay?”

“Yeah.”

“We’ll go look at the apartment in Pembroke together after I get done.”

“Okay. How much are they asking?”

“Seventeen hundred. Between the two of us and the Needy Families we should be able to make it, Sid.”

“Okay. If you say so.”

“I know so. I got it figured out. And the apartment is right next to the school for her. She'd be dying to go to school.”

Ruth dropped Sid off first in the parking lot of the Market Basket. The parking lot was still dark, but the lights were on in the store. Sid pushed his way through the automatic doors. There were people moving quickly around and the sound of machinery in the back somewhere. Sid looked around for Tony V, the Produce Department manager who’d interviewed him three days ago. He walked around in the produce section, trying to stay out of the way of the workers pushing crates of fruit and vegetables around the aisles. They were chatting to each other. Sid walked to the back and saw Tony V.

“Oh, yeah. Hey Sid,” said Tony V. He was about mid-forty, with blackened teeth. He moved quickly. Sid stayed right with him as they went back to the loading docks, and Tony V showed Sid the buffing machine. It was charged every morning in a closet, so that it was ready to go. You just had to put fresh discs on it every other day. And remember to use the red ones, not the blue ones, except on waxing days, which occurred at the beginning and middle of every month. But Tony V would be in charge of letting him know what mornings that would be. So that was no worry. Everything was dead easy, too easy, thought Sid. Tony V showed Sid where the boxes of discs were kept, in another section of the back rooms, just before you went through into the freezers. The trick was getting the floors buffed whenever the assistants were done with the initial set up and before the doors opened. You had about a twenty to thirty minute window, he explained.

Tony V walked behind Sid that first day for the first few minutes, until he thought Sid had a handle on how to run the machine. Then Sid was on his own.

The rhythm of the work was pleasant enough. He liked the way the discs cut through some of the built up stains that lined the aisles in front of the rubber molding. He liked the way the floor came up looking shiny and fresh after the buffing. It fit his idea of what a reasonable sort of work entailed, harmless and focused on surfaces. Sid liked the fluorescent light of the aisles and the freshly misted rows of pears, pumpkins, bok choy, and rows of greens of the produce section. He liked the chatter of the associates and the fact that they left him alone to do his job. Afterwards, he plugged the floor buffer back on its dock in the back room. He checked the disc for its condition. Tony V called him into his office with a desk overflowing with notebooks and hastily scribbled receipts.

"How'd you do?" asked Tony V, shutting the door behind him. "It's fucking crazy here," he added.

"Yeah. I like it," said Sid.

"That's good. That's good. Listen, I need you to fill out the W-2 for me."

"Oh, yeah. Fine," said Sid.

Tony V pushed the form to the corner of the desk nearest Sid. Then he got out from behind the desk and let Sid sit down.

"What should I do when I'm done?"

"Come find me. We'll need some boxes moved into the freezer."

Sid filled out the form, nervous about some of the questions. He left the questions unanswered where he was unsure. He signed it uncertainly and fidgeted with where to leave it before dropping it in the middle of the desk. He pulled out the drawer. There was a bottle of Percocets in the back, just like he thought there would be. Sid felt the plastic bottle between his index finger and thumb and read the label. He took out a fat pill, examined it, and swallowed it down, put the bottle back, and closed the desk drawer. Soon enough he was feeling all right with the world. He found Tony V, who set Sid and a young, acne-faced guy named Wayne to stack boxes of avocados from the loading dock into the freezer. Wayne was a January graduate of a high school on the other side of Manchester. Sid decided he was quiet because people must have told him he was dumb from an early age. He got him talking about bass fishing, the sport he liked the best. Sid wanted to help Wayne develop more confidence. Wayne was prone to hanging back in his interactions. He did a very good impression of casting for bass in the shallows of Stumpfield Pond where Route 9 went overhead. Sid let him take the lead stacking the boxes up on the shelves, while Sid slid them across to the door of the freezer. The cold air of the freezer let out a cloud of fog, as Sid held it open. Wayne's thin body almost disappeared in the fog.

After stacking the avocado boxes, Sid hung out on the loading dock listening to a couple of the truck drivers chatting with three female associates. Then he glanced at Tony V walking through the loading dock and smiled.

"You done with the avocado boxes?" asked Tony V.

"Oh yeah," said Sid.

"You done for today. Punch out. We'll see you tomorrow?"

"Yeah. Of course," said Sid, projecting the appropriate amount of laid back confidence, he thought.

"Same time," said Tony V.

Sid walked up to the Pacha Mama. He and Ruth drove out to Pembroke and looked at an apartment above the town in a new development. The agent was distracted. She looked like she'd been asleep somewhere. She wasn't much help to them as they tried to figure out how much it would come to after deposits and fees. There were nice, solid cabinets in the kitchen that opened and closed on a glide the way they were supposed to, but it seemed a little beyond their budget at the moment. There were fees for the parking that Ruth hadn't counted on. They drove away back to the Pacha Mama, stopping at the gas station at Bow Junction. Ruth ate a salad from the gas station in the car on the second floor in the parking garage. Sid finished his chicken sandwich. He swigged from a white bottle of a caffeinated energy drink.

"It's not great. We gotta find something, Sid."

"We'll just keep looking. Maybe there's a place we can find somewhere. Out in the country, above someone's barn. Word of mouth," said Sid. He was still feeling good, riding the Percocet express.

"Yeah, maybe," said Ruth. "Some place with chickens, Right, Sid?"

"That's right," said Sid.

That night, it was Sid's turn to cook something. He left the heat up too high for a minute while he opened a beer, and the aluminum pan overheated. The fried eggs got a little burnt on the edges before he had a chance to flip them. The spaghetti clumped together in the camping pot. Leesha wanted mashed potatoes instead, so Ruth found some leftovers all the way in the back of the refrigerator, wrapped in some tin foil. Leesha was grumpy and whiny. She'd had some bad dreams. Fears of people hiding under her bed and trying to hurt her. She had her own small mattress in the bedroom the three of them shared. Boyle heated up some noodles in the microwave while they ate.

"Here you go, Leesh. Try these," said Ruth.

"They hot?" asked Leesha.

"No. Do you want me to warm them up?" asked Ruth.

"Yes, please."

"Don't spoil her," said Boyle.

"Are you done with that?" asked Ruth, pointing to the microwave. It dinged. Boyle removed the pot of noodles.

"Nothing wrong with this," said Sid, holding up the clumped spaghetti on his fork. Leesha wouldn't look at him. "Mmmm," he said, sticking the forkful in his mouth. Leesha tried to smile.

"Just trying to get her to eat so she'll sleep tonight, Boyle," said Ruth.

"Just normal kid stuff, right?" said Boyle.

"She just needs a better day-time situation. School would be nice," said Ruth.

"You wanna go to school, Leesh?" asked Boyle from the door, spooning noodles into his mouth.

Leesha looked over at him and made a pouting face.

"You should see where I'm working. The old people. Something wrong with the country that don't take care of the very young or the very old," said Boyle. "I try to do my best for them, but sometimes, man, it just gets to be too much. There's only so much one person can do. I mean, the stink alone. It's unbearable in some of the rooms. Nobody changes the sheets, nobody gets them up and gets them moved around, which we're under contract for. But nobody cares."

"It's just a job, Boyle," said Sid.

Boyle was a person who carried around a lot of simmering anger at the way people were. He kept talking about moving to Europe. He liked the way people were over there, which Sid thought was absolute madness. It would either wear him down or he'd end up in the correctional facility. Sid made a note to try to figure out how to steer Boyle straight. After eating, they all sat in the living room while Boyle played the guitar. Leesha played with a couple of dolls. Rover tried to get them away from her. He was feeling playful and wouldn't stop stealing the dolls, so Sid put him outside. Just then, a plain white van drove up and parked behind Lesli's car, the Focus, and Boyle's Ridgeline truck. Sid watched from the open front door as Peter got out of the driver's side and Lesli popped out on the passenger side. Lesli seemed even more subdued than usual, laughing carefully at something Peter said. Sid imagined he wasn't the funniest guy in the world, just watching him come up the drive. He immediately got a bad feeling from him when Rover came up and Peter swung a foot at the dog, trying to kick him half-heartedly. Sid didn't say anything, just kept the door open and waited for the two to climb the steps. Inside the house, Boyle and Ruth were singing a song. Ruth stopped singing and yelled at them to close the door. They were letting too much cold air in.

"Hi, Sid. This is Peter. Mah boyfriend," said Lesli, sounding drunk.

“Hi,” said Sid.

“How you doin’, Sid,” said Peter. He stuck his hand out. Sid shook his hand. Peter gripped Sid’s hand like a steel trap. Sid smiled. He was at least half a head taller. Lesli pushed by the two of them to the inside.

“You visiting for a few days?” asked Peter.

“Yeah, something like that,” said Sid.

“That’s cool,” said Peter. “Boy, it’s cold up here,” he added. He shouldered past Sid into the house. Peter closed the door behind him. Sid walked down the steps into the snow behind the house. He could see Rover running in the woods back towards him. Behind him he could see the people in the living room greeting each other and settling back on the two old sofas while Boyle perched on one of the birch stumps with a guitar by his side.

Sid was struck by the sight. It seemed like it should have been a bigger deal to be standing out in the snow looking at people mulling about inside a provisionally warm shelter, while the dog stretched out and wriggled on his back in the snow. And yet, this string of moments, reflected in his mind, was numbly observed as if through a gauzy curtain. He felt his mind was going to suddenly become unblocked and feared that the movie he was watching would begin to stream faster and faster, becoming a blur to him, leaving him outside for good. It was like a glacier untouched by warming currents since Meg’s death, guarded from the swirling mess of life that picked you up and shut you down. Sometimes he thought Meg had died in a vain attempt to break through to this same unmoved mind of his, the block of stone that had looked at the world from the earliest age, from beyond a time in his memory. And all the time, since he could remember, Sid had been trying to see if he could somehow change it, shape it like Steve shaped stone and wood. Drugs, women, jail, prayer, and now, the same mind that observed life as if underwater, that had come back time after time, a mutant regrowth, suggested to him the futility of everything you could do to try to mold your life. At the end of the day you were stuck with your same detached, numbheaded self. What was the point? You grew up, you tried to get yourself in a place so that you could take care of things with a minimal amount of fuss in a system that was bent on destroying your soul. And what was a soul? It was just the same mind coming back time after time to the same conclusions, the same detached coolness that was only a little different than dying.

Dying couldn't be bad, thought Sid depending on how you did it. Stepping down from the arena of life, going down all the paths he'd taken. All he'd ever wanted was to feel something.

Meg was the beginning and end of everything. Thinking of her caused this pile-on of regret -- his lack of feeling compounded by loss of memory. He'd been to prison, served his time, but nothing erased the sting of her face and youth. The waste of their lives. If he had killed her, he really deserved more than nineteen years in the correctional facility. But he hadn't. Not killed. Not Meg. He was sure of that. Otherwise how was it that he had surfaced as if from another life by the riverbank, and seen the canoe sweeping downstream, towards the turbulent white water passage on its side, taking on water and nobody in the bow where she should have been? He had seen it. And how had he clambered along the rocks, walking upstream calling her name, climbing the banks in a pounding daze as if concussed, stopping the pickup truck with the two rock climbers on their way to the Kancamagus?

The police found her a few miles ahead, washed up under the highway bridge. That afternoon they arrested him, took him into custody. At the trial, the rock climbers testified to his disturbed mental state, witnesses for the defense, but the prosecuting attorney had pressed them, got them to admit that Sid seemed able to recall details from the canoe trip, from where they had set out, at what time. He still remembered what she had in her backpack: the PSU sweatshirt, bottle of tanning lotion, thermos of water, the journal with her drawings, ticket receipt to the Phish concert in Burlington, and the three rolled joints in the cough drop tin.

It was so convoluted that there was no way to sort it out. The best advice he'd been able to get from the counselor in the correctional facility, who came twice in every three month block, was to trust in time to heal the wounds. But all time did was numb out your feelings, rot any humanity you had left after nineteen years in the correctional facility like a stack of wood left on the side of a shack in Loonberg.

Time was the enemy, Sid thought. Accepting the illusion of the passage of time, accepting that there was no escape. Really, he needed to move quickly and get to the bottom of the puzzle, even if it meant flailing like he was. The worst thing was to sit back quietly and accept this string of meaninglessness that added up to a so-called life. That was Sid's true enemy.

There was no such thing as time. Time was just an idea that had been invented in order to extract compliance. Do your time and you will be free. The whole thing was a hoax. There was no time and nobody could set you free. Only you could free your mind. But how? Meg was dead. Time had stopped and the idea of freedom had died with her.

Peter had been in South Carolina. He'd been working on a roofing crew in Charlotte. They were Proud Boys and wannabee podcasters. Some of them were okay, but most of them just wanted to party. Not like him. He was trying to get back with Prudholme in Candia. They always needed people with experience, and business was picking up. Roofing was a great job because you could go anywhere. Sid didn't say it, but he didn't trust himself up on a roof. He liked the floor buffing job. It gave him time to think and he didn't need to depend on anybody else. The machine was low maintenance, and eventually he could work his way up to full-time associate and get health care. In the meantime, he was in the market for a cheap car, he announced. Peter didn't drive anything but a truck, or in his present situation, a commercial van, he said. It was below his dignity to drive an ordinary sedan, or even to consider what that was like, the advantages of gas mileage.

The van, Lesli explained, while Peter was in the bathroom, was a loaner from an uncle in Croydon while he worked on getting his truck back from repossession. A van, said Peter, settling back down on the sofa next to Lesli with that confidence of his, was preferable to some smaller car. Sid thought maybe Peter hadn't figured out the marketing ploy involved in putting those ideas in their heads. Sid was going to get into it with him, but Boyle went there first.

"So what you're thinking is a commuter car usually means you look like a wimp, right?" said Boyle.

"No. Not necessarily. Just not for me, that's all. I like to have the capability."

"Sling your tools back in there," said Boyle.

"Whatever," said Peter. "Give me a van or a truck."

"Nobody's giving you anything," said Lesli, laughing nervously.

Ruth and Sid went to bed, leaving Boyle, Lesli and Peter in the living room. Leesha was asleep on her mattress. They tried not to wake her as they undressed and lay down. It was cold. There was no heat in the house besides the wood stove in the living room. At least they had each other. Sid thrilled at the feel of her back and shoulders. He ran his hand along her buttocks. They squeezed tighter together and then slowly made love. The intensity of their arousal was due partly to the need for quiet in the full house with thin walls and Leesha asleep at their feet. She was under a couple of sleeping bags, but even so, their efforts were less than silent. Sid thought afterwards he would always remember Ruth's eyes in the light of the stars through the crack in the curtains, her bared teeth like some hungry animal.

The next day, Sid noticed the buffing machine had the wrong color disc on it. The evening shift must have done something different. He found a new red disc in the closet next to the charging dock and placed it back on the machine. He had the machine ready to go, and looked out through the plastic dividing screen to see when the assistants were beginning to clear out from the produce section. There was still some movement, scurrying back and forth through the divider. The bustle left Sid feeling empty, disconnected. It struck him as obscene, the mottled, waxy hues of green avocados and red apples in such profusion. He retreated to Tony V's office. The sun was just beginning to light up the sky. Sid reached quickly into the drawer, removed the bottle of Percocets, unscrewed the cap and shook out a pill into his palm. There were still plenty left in the bottle. Sid knew what he was doing was wrong, but he didn't care. There was something wrong with the pills that reached out to the part that was wrong with Sid. The mutual attraction between the two wrongs made it right somehow. The pill gave Sid a peace of mind. It relaxed him, took the edge off of his experience of the world and his fellow workers.

Thanks to the pills, Sid made it through the day. The next morning, Sid went into the office straightaway and noticed the bottle sitting on the desk. He thought that was strange, but his idea of a pill was set firmly enough that it overrode the caution signals going off in his mind. He shook out a pill and downed it. Tangerines, broccoli and pears. They were all alright by Sid. He wanted the floor to look perfect. He wanted his job to reflect his self-worth, and the produce section to be an image of the bounty that was everyone's due.

Tony V called him into the office when he was cleaning up, half way through the morning. Sid was coiling the extension cord.

"You almost done?" asked Tony V.

"Yeah."

"Whenever you're done. There's no hurry," said Tony V.

That should do it, he thought, hanging the cord up on its hook. The sun was lighting up the sky in the loading area. It promised to be a clear, blazing blue, Pilgrim sky. He went into the office. Tony V was talking with one of the female associates. They both turned around and glanced sideways at Sid. The female associate said one or two more things and left. Tony V went and leaned against the desk.

"How are you, Sid?'

"Good," said Sid, rubbing his hands to keep them warm.

"Listen, it's not going to happen here, Sid."

"What's that?"

"You working here. Not going to happen."

"Why not?" said Sid. He felt like something had struck him in the side of the head, like a canoe capsizing and hitting the white water.

"I'm not going to get into it. Just get your stuff and leave."

"You're not giving me a reason."

"I don't have to."

"Well, that sucks."

Tony V just stared at him with an expressionless face. He looked like a lizard with the gray skin of a dying man.

"I was counting on this."

"I understand."

"You don't understand shit."

"No, hold on. Listen," said Tony V, feigning pain.

"I uh, do I get paid for today?"

"Of course. I'll cut you a check right now."

"I want cash."

"We don't pay in cash."

"If I don't get cash I'm going to light it up around here."

Sid's agitated demeanor with the bolded, Percocet-inspired tone of his words seemed to convince Tony V to take him seriously.

"Okay. Wait here. I'll see what I can do," he said.

While he was out, Sid lifted the bottle of Percocets and stuck it in his coat pocket, where it settled along with the brochure for Oxford Health that was almost unrecognizable, a sedimentary deposit of Sid's already largely forgotten past. Tony V returned. He left the door to the office open behind him and shouted some joke to a passing bunch of associates from the other departments.

"Busy today," he said.

Sid stayed quiet.

Tony V counted out the five twenty dollar bills on the desk and added three singles. He lifted the wad up to Sid.

"Here you go, buddy."

"Thanks," mumbled Sid.

“Sorry it didn’t work out. Nothing personal,” said Tony V.

Sid stayed quiet. There was nothing personal. Ever. Only what you made it. Whenever they said there was nothing personal, there usually was something hidden to ordinary people that contradicted that meaning. Sid reflected on the slippery nature of language as he walked up the hill to Main Street. So much came out in the intonations that were hidden from plain sense. How were they ever going to program robots to do anything? A robot would never know enough to walk away from Tony V’s office and maintain a semblance of dignity. A robot would never be able to deal with the duplicity that was in the nature of words, perhaps even in the nature of the human mind.

The weather was warming. Snow banks receded along the streets. Shoppers were out on the sidewalks and the homeless people were beginning to sprout in doorways, unfurling like ferns. Sid walked along, sniffing out meaning like a dog from the air, from glances, snatches of conversation, from the music coming from the food trucks. This was freedom, basking in the relevance of the moment, lifting one foot after another, unstoppable. He reached the end of Main Street and turned around. Sid believed that his prayers went out to life, to the spirit world. The vigor he felt all went to his head, but sometimes life answered.

When he saw Bernier’s girlfriend coming out of the New England Gift Shop and head into Joe King’s, at first it didn’t register. He followed inside the store, just to check.

He walked alongside as she looked at the row of leather boots. It was her. She looked around and saw him staring. Sid looked away and picked up a pair of shoes. He felt her approach, and instead of tensing he seemed oddly relaxed.

"Hi, Sid. Need some clogs?"

"Hi. Yeah, not really." He put the clogs back.

"Funny world, isn't it?" she said.

"I forget your name."

"That's okay. Carissa."

"What's your last name?"

"Jackson."

"We were never introduced. How are things with Bernier?"

"Don't ask. It's in the rear view mirror. Know what I mean?"

"What about the sheep?"

"Yeah. Funny, isn't it? Sheep. How about you? Everything going well?"

Sid was quiet. He reflected that quite possibly she was more confused than he at this coincidental recurrence, this overlap in their paths. He should try and help her, he thought. That was the obvious way forward.

"I'm figuring out which way to take myself. I liked working up there in Gilford, though, with all the guys."

"I'm sure you can get plenty of work. You were a good worker. That wall was a beauty."

"Thanks."

"Well, what are you doing with yourself nowadays?"

"I'm not sure." Sid picked up another pair of shoes. "I like cleaning. There's something very satisfying about it."

"That's good, Sid," said Carissa, nodding. "It's nice to be satisfied like that."

"It's clean, simple. Not like most people. You know?"

"Got to look out for number one," she agreed.

"But it kind of sucks at the same time. There's a lot of work I need to do on myself," said Sid.

"Tell me about it. I know."

"Hey, I liked some of the books in your bookshelf in the guesthouse. I liked Italo what's his name."

"Calvino."

"Yeah him."

"What did you like about it?"

"I don't know. Just the stories. I liked the way they just rambled on."

"Yeah. Convoluted. Like real life."

"I like stories like that. It gets you out of your own misery."

"So. What are you doing now?" she asked, glancing around.

"Right now? I'm talking to you in this shoe store."

"You want to take a ride?"

"Where you going?"

"I don't know. We'll flip a coin."

"Well, I'm willing. Let's flip a coin and see," Sid smiled.

"Anywhere, really."

"Absolutely."

Carissa stopped on the sidewalk in front of a white BMW. Sid could feel his heart racing. Something beeped and the doors opened a crack on both sides.

"Get in, Sid," she said.

Sid sat in the car. The seat sucked him down. He leaned back into the new, padded leather.

"Do you want to drive?" she asked. He looked over at her and studied her face, the straight lines of the nose and cheeks, the way her hair curled around her ears.

"No, that's okay."

"Just sit back and relax then, Sid."

"Where are we going?"

"I don't know. Let's play a game. I'll mention a word and you tell me the first thing that comes into your mind."

"Okay."

"Lemon."

"Tree."

"Very good. Ice."

"Water."

"Very suggestive. Okay. One more. You name a word."

"I don't know. Road."

"Freedom," said Carissa.

"From what?" asked Sid.

"Let's find out."

They drove south for a couple of hours and ended up winding around silently on the streets somewhere in Boston. Carissa looked over at him. Sid had been silent, his thoughts kept to himself.

"We're here. Home."

"Free," said Sid.

"I wish," she laughed.

"We made it," said Sid.

"I'm like a homing pigeon. I just flew back here, Sid. Is that okay?"

"Yeah," said Sid. "It's okay by me."

Sid was so hungry he could hardly think. He slipped himself two Percocets.

He couldn't help turning things over in his mind, looking for an advantage. He realized it was selfish. But then again, life had not ever been a straight shot for him. Even now, there was nothing simple. Everything depended on how it was interpreted. Carissa was sharp, way out of his league, which suggested pain and humiliation. But everything about her was shining, with clean angles that promised possibility, a world of possibility heretofore alien to his existence.

Carissa parked in the basement of a complex. She had an apartment in this building. The security guards chatting in the booth didn't look at either of them. Sid got the feeling they were the first people to ever have entered the building. It was like a chapel. The glass and mirrored surfaces they glimpsed as the elevator doors opened automatically on the ground floor seemed like a mirage. She carried some of her shopping, some boutique bags and an antique lamp. Sid offered to carry the lamp, and she handed it to him wordlessly. They got off the elevator in a hallway of muted lights and paper thin vases on a marble table.

"This is it," she said. "My cave."

Carissa opened her door with the swipe of a security card. She seemed oddly apprehensive, as if she feared Sid would somehow judge her. Sid stopped in the middle of the floor and looked around. The apartment was stuffed with furniture, tapestries, and assorted modernist porcelain bric a brac. It seemed a little overdone to Sid, but he thought there was probably more to the decor than he could appreciate.

"Make yourself comfortable. Do you want something to eat?"

"What do you have?"

"I'm not sure. Why don't you look in the fridge?"

Sid opened the refrigerator. There was a bottle of pomegranate juice, a plastic bag of baby carrots, and a paper bag of old bagels. Sid took a bagel and ate it raw, shoving it down his throat. Carissa appeared in a bathrobe. Sid shut the refrigerator door. He tried to smile as he finished swallowing.

"Actually, why don't you come in and have a bath, Sid."

"A bath?"

"Yeah. You'll like it. I'll run a bath for you. And I'll order some food."

Carissa led him into a bathroom lined with mirrors on the wall and ceiling. The bathtub had ornamental legs in the shape of an imaginary animal's paws. She ran the water and poured in some bath salts. Sid watched her with curiosity and some apprehension. This was nice, but unexpected. It was such an echo of some fantasy that he could only wonder what was the catch.

"Did you ever see the movie *The Last Tango in Paris*, Sid?"

"No."

"There's a scene in there between Marlon Brando and Maria Schneider. He plays this American who wants to forget everything about his past. That reminds me of you."

"Why?"

"There's like a blankness to you, Sid."

"Okay. I don't want to forget the past, though."

"Are you sure you don't?"

"No. I'm not sure. Maybe I do. I don't know."

"Go ahead, get in. It's ready now."

"Really?"

"Yeah, take off your clothes and get in. It's nice and warm." She laughed.

"Don't laugh at me."

"I'm not laughing at you, Sid."

He took off his clothes and got in. The water and soap slid up his body. It felt good. His mood seemed to lighten, as if the water had washed away the inevitability of loss.

"Is that nice?" She called from outside the bathroom.

"Yeah."

She came back into the bathroom. Her facial expression had changed slightly. She looked worried now.

"What's happening?' asked Sid.

"Not much," she said.

"Are you getting in?" asked Sid bravely.

"Why? Do you want me to?" she asked, hesitantly.

"Sure."

"You seem sad."

"Okay."

"Are you sure you want me to, Sid?"

"No. I'm not sure of anything. But do it anyway."

She smiled and began to undress, shedding her clothes on the floor. Then she slipped into the bathtub, letting the water slowly slide up her body like a blanket. She closed her eyes. He felt her feet touch his privates, and he began to get an erection.

"We don't need this, do we Sid? It's so passe."

Her feet massaged him as she spoke. He reached forward and cupped her breasts.

"Is that what it's all about?"

"Yeah," said Sid.

"Do you want me to be quiet? I can be quiet, or I can keep talking."

"Keep talking."

Sid was on his knees. He felt the dirt sliding off of him in the greasy bath water. They made love in the bathtub. Sid blanked out.

When he came to his senses, spitting and thrashing, she was watching him, both hands up around her face as if she was a boxer, readying a strike.

"You got your hands around my neck," she said, coughing. "That was some weird shit, Sid."

Sid sat back and held his breath. He studied her eyes.

"No. That's just not true."

"Yes, it is."

Sid slapped her across the face.

She stared at him, horrified, then pulled herself out of the water. Sid held his breath.

She came back in, wrapped in a towel.

"What is your problem?" she asked. She'd been crying.

Sid felt so damaged and full of pain. She was going to take pity on him but thought better of it.

"You'll have to go. I don't want to see you here. Do you understand?"

"Yeah."

"I thought I could help you. You scared me. I don't trust you now. I want you out. Get dressed and get out."

"You don't have to say it like that. I understand."

Sid got out of the bath. The water was cold. He was shivering. He dried off and got dressed. She was nowhere to be seen. He was at the door when she spoke from the sofa.

"Good bye, Sid."

She seemed like the loneliest person he'd ever seen, even if he was the one going out the door.

"I'm sorry," he said.

The door closed. Sid watched it latch and imagined Carissa on the sofa staring at her door. They were on opposite sides now, lines reestablished. For a second, he felt her disappointment as it flooded his mind. He turned and hit the button for the elevator.

V - Mt. Auburn

Sid walked along in the early night until he reached the Charles River. There were joggers and groups of Chinese women in twill coats and slow boats in the black water. A cold wind blew in from the city to the east and the ocean. A line of indigo extended along the horizon until it met a spreading pool of blood-red light at the western fringe of the skyline. Fragments of conversation mixed with the low whine of traffic. Sid felt the numb certainty of a hopeless soul set adrift in an ocean of consciousness, recognizing the folly of twilit remembrance. He stopped halfway out on the bridge over the river and looked down at the swirling water.

If he was going to go, he wanted somebody to know his thoughts. He had nobody to unburden himself to. That seemed to be a stupid point of pride, but it was enough of a stumbling block. Even the voices of his dreams seemed to admonish him. He couldn't end it before he'd had a chance to expose himself fully to another human being. What he had found out with Carissa was that it was a longer term project than anybody knew. It was hard work. Knowing the truth, now that he knew the truth, was not any easier. On the contrary, it just got a lot more complicated. Even when he made love, or especially when he made love, he was at his most wrecked. He probably had always known that. He had probably always known he'd killed her, the girl that was going to save him. Meg'd been the first to go down the rabbit hole with him. But far from finding the Queen of Hearts, Sid always came up with the Joker. He guessed he'd always known that about himself also. Love was a double-edged sword. It took love, subtracted it from you, and created a deficit which made you lash out in secret rage. And everybody was possibly involved in the same, hare-brained scheme of mutual destruction, just as murderous as he was. Which was the reason the world was such a topsy-turvy store of pandemonium, constantly going off the rails, stains of sin spreading like oil sheen across the pristine water.

He didn't want to kill anybody. But everybody he touched ended up, if not dead, then haunted. The only rescue possible from the water, from the cold oblivion below, was to seclude himself away and try to lance the poison through self-medication and suffering. There was no going back to the people who promised to love and care for him. Happy people were generous, kind, forgiving and selfless. Unhappy people were angry, vindictive and spiteful. Sid observed that unhappiness was the default human condition. The downside of this observation was that happiness was some kind of artifact, propped up by conditions that were unknown to Sid and a conspiracy of some elite kind.

So he walked the streets through the night, never stopping, pursued by grief and the relentless need to escape a destruction that seemed to dog him. He would whirl and try to catch the demons in the act. Cops and robbers of the brain. But there was nobody there. Always watchful eyes followed his movements. There was a collective judgement afoot, shifting slightly in barely perceptible ways. At a shop somewhere on Massachusetts Avenue, he went in through the glass doors, pulling them aside clumsily. The heat vent above the door came on and whirred a blast of hot air down on his head. Sid removed his cap and stamped his feet. A man came in behind him, a little man in a peacoat and dark pools under his eyes. He had old tennis shoes and baggy sweatpants. Sid bought a cheese sandwich from the deli section and a bottle of iced coffee. He moved down the sidewalk, watch cap pulled tightly down around his ears. He didn't want to hear anything that could intrude and confuse him. From a doorway, he propped himself and watched.

The little man came out and turned past him. Sid chewed loudly and mumbled to himself. An ambulance went by, siren blaring.

My heart sank when I first saw you. Of course I knew it was you even though you'd never seen me. The captains brought you in a company of new men and dumped you inside the gate, sent you sprawling in the mud with your boots and coat and the rest of us looking on, hanging on the new arrivals, searching out weaknesses unseen by merely human eyes. The stockade closed slowly like a mountain on the circles of hell behind you and some of the sentries in the nearest watchtowers fired off rounds in the air overhead to let us know once again who was the boss of this Golgotha. I followed your eyes as you studied the layout of the yard, going as far afield as you could stretch from where you sat up on the bluff, like a chick in a field of grass on the first warm day of the summer, ignorant of the black birds of prey circling in the pine trees. I sat on the opposite bank with Colonel Wormington, both of us puffing pipes stuffed with rations of old newsprint, pages of the Macon Telegraph and stalks of grass we'd saved up from the last days of fall.

'Who're they? Greenhorns if I'd never seen,' said the Colonel.

'Men of the 1st New Hampshire, sir. They say they were among the prisoners taken at Little Bull Run. Been pirated through Ohio and down Arkansas by the 12th Virginia,' I said.

I had all the latest intelligence. My eyes and ears were like a spiderweb laying over the cursed twenty six acres of that foul prison.

'Better for them if they'd never seen the Georgia winter,' said Wormington.

It went on raining like a swollen river letting itself go for a good week. You stopped caring about the mud and the stench. Three of your fellows died inside that week. That left ten or so of you in the hole you'd taken. I followed your eyes when the stockade doors opened and the crowd surged, hollowed-out eye sockets and stumps of bare boned digits cadging for the stale bread and rotted cabbages tossed onto the ground for sport as if we were foraging animals.

You didn't disappoint. You sprinted past the lumbering bodies, managed three black cabbages into your coat and quickly scoured the ground for the cornbread which you scraped with your fingers and stuffed in your mouth as if you'd had a plan. But I knew you, of course. That quickness and nimbleness had made you a favorite of father's and would stand you in good stead in Andersonville.

Before you reached the tent you'd been waylaid by three of the Raiders. We stood on the banks to see. The snow drifted down over the scene, turning the puddles of rotten water silver. One of the Raiders clubbed you over the head, and they took the cabbages from you as you fell to your knees. They kicked you and had a few words with you where you lay face down. Then they were gone. You had no choice. In order to survive you would have to join the stronger force or die. Wormington didn't know that I had recognized you.

'That boy's gonna die sure as hell,' said the colonel.

'Not unless we can get to him first,' I said.

'Why would we do that?'

'He's my brother.'

'That's a weight that don't hold water here, Bill.'

'No. He's my actual brother. That's Joe Welch. He's only sixteen, I reckon.'

Wormington puffed on his pipe judiciously. Every move in the camp had to be sifted three times in at least four dimensions. This was where I trusted Wormington. His eyes saw deeper than anybody into the marrow of existence, the secrets that extended back in time, beyond birth and death and the span of any one man's given life, as if his eyes were privy to scenes beyond the ken of mortals. Colonel Worminton had a high pitched voice like a woman's. Sometimes I suspected he was a shapeshifter, an actual ghost come to life in this haunted place so as to confuse and lay the rails for a higher plot that would only prevail in hindsight. Wormington claimed he was an officer of the Vermont 172nd Brigade, mustered out of Bennington, but I'd never met anybody else who could say they'd served with him. It was an incongruity I largely ignored, especially at times like these, when I needed the assurance of superior insight.

'Better have a word with him, then,' said the Colonel. It was what I wanted to hear.

I waited. For patience was a virtue that knew no bounds in the camp. Most of the time we waited. The rebels knew that time was not on their side. We used to taunt the sentries, yelling about their women folk in danger.

'Hurry home, rebs, before it's too late. No tellin' what those boys get up to in your stead. They say the beds a creakin' like hell, your wives and daughters a humpin' along goin' nowhere fast,' we yelled, or words to that effect. And then watch out and take cover as the vindictive and troubled men, tools of their Tidewater masters, fired into the crowd, picking off a few poor devils that would roll slowly over and tumble into the border ditch along the wall. Probably better off that way. The camp was so overcrowded that some of us welcomed a few square inches of extra breathing room and sighed with pleasure at the sight of those men gone to an untimely and unforgettable grave, for it meant a better likelihood of canvas overhead in the still freezing nights of March.

When I reached your side, days had gone by since your first acquaintance with Camp Sumter. You were hungry. Every time you took food on your own you were tackled by someone with a club.

They were slowly taking your life. You would have no choice. Any minute you would seek them out and fall to your knees, begging for a scrap, just another casualty of the system that operated in the camp. The Raiders took what they needed, and their enemies, those who refused to bend their knee and accept what they were allotted, could only perish. Some played the odds and accepted the punishment of beatings and social ostracism as long as they could. They ended up wraiths, and then they were gone. A few, only a select few, organized into a resistance that relied on secrecy of an extreme kind and a cleverness that could hide as solidarity. I tried to explain all this to you from your side as we watched men scurrying and lolling slowly in groups, in the round of routine chores and ablutions that occupied their days.

'How long have you been here, Bill, just watching me like you say?'

'Since you got here. Why didn't you stay home and take care of mother like you were supposed to?'

'She's fine. She can take care of herself. Why didn't you say something if you saw me?'

'I had to take my time. The Raiders don't know who they've got to contend with. They just know that they are not in charge. They don't have the complete control they claim or would like. And you are going to play your part, Joe. This is what father would have wanted. Don't you worry.'

'But that's a fool's part, Bill. There's only one thing to do and that's make a run for it.'

'Nobody's ever,' I said.

'There's two of us now. Hell, nothing can hold us back, Bill. Not even this shithole.'

There were two of us, and where there were two of the Welches the entire world could cave and spring afresh. Anything was possible when looked at in that way, but I was unsure, fearful of your excessive pride. Our father would surely give us counsel and tell us to keep our heads down and wait for spring. But you were having none of it. You were all for bounding up then and there and had a way of convincing me, despite my greater number of years. Caution will always give way to the greater energy of a vision, even when the proof of calamity is spread right there for all to see.

You took food. Marcus Benjamin, the head of the Raiders, fed you and sheltered you in his tent, and in exchange you became a runner, taking messages to the prison captains on the outside, passing freely over the boundary ditch, recognized by the sentries, legs sturdy with your diet of cabbage and pork rind and stale cornbread. Once in a while, every other day or so I managed to catch up to you for a few words. You'd let me know what Benjamin's thoughts had recently concluded, and I passed that information along to Wormington and the secret resisters that acted as a vigilante judiciary. Benjamin knew that there were informants among his men and shuffled them like a deck of cards. Your usefulness had an expiry date. I tried to explain that to you, in as few words as I could manage.

'You've done a heck of a job, Joe. Nobody's taking that away from you. But one day you will hear a whistling noise and it's the last thing you'll hear,' I said.

'You don't seem to appreciate the position I'm in, though. I'm going in and out of the gates. I'm on good terms with Commander Wirz.'

'Of course I appreciate it. They say he has a wooden leg.'

'That's not true. He just walks with difficulty due to a bullet he took fighting the Bohemian uprising for the Hapsburg prince.'

'Is that so?'

'I have it on good authority.'

'Shit. You're getting too full of yourself. Fly too close to Wirz and you'll be burnt up. I've seen it before,' I said, lying. Nobody had ever found the story of Wirz's injuries before.

'What can I do, Bill? I have to eat.'

'We all do. Does he intend to let us starve?'

'There is no other plan.'

'And the Raiders? What does Benjamin intend?'

'He most certainly don't care. It's every man for hisself. Benjamin runs the Raiders to keep it going until Sherman can reach us. Atlanta has already been liberated. There is a plan afoot, he assures me, but does not dare whisper it to a soul. But we need to go, Bill. You and me. NOW!'

'I'm not sure how far I can hold out. Another week or two and I'll be useless.'

'Tonight. Meet me right here at midnight. I'll wait.'

I looked at you long and hard. It was all in vain, but together it would be worth the candle. I shivered and felt feverish.

'I'll bring the rope,' I said.

The rope was made from the undershirts of dead men, tied together to form a cord about twenty yards long. It was coiled under Colonel Wormington, who slept with it at night. It was our prized possession. He gave me his blessing and his diary, written on Spanish rice paper and folded into a neat bundle that could fit in the palm of your hand. He told me to take it and deliver it to the proper authorities when I could.

'You'll see to it that the world understands what we have endured,' said the Colonel.

'I will do my best,' I said.

'Then you can do no worse,' said the Colonel, kissing me.

I lifted the flap and went out, carrying the rope under my sack coat and my personal papers folded up along with the Colonel's diary in a handkerchief I kept under my regimental cap. Pairs of eyes barely registered my passing in the darkness. The wind had picked up and was blowing a stiff, cold air from the North. That was perfect, as it would ensure the sentries doing night duty would keep low, hunkered down in their towers to shelter from the cold. The whistling wind would also prevent any noise from being easily heard. The ruses of the night are a balm to the heart of the refugee.

You were there, kneeling on the bluff in the attitude of a Mussulman praying to his Mecca. I climbed up the slight rise from behind and lay beside you, pulling my cap tight. The only light in the night sky was the great Milky Way from behind thick clouds. We were in a small clearing, surrounded by the field of men spread out before us, littered with tents and bodies huddled together in the open, sometimes dead, many times in that grey area behind life and death, like distant cousins at a family gathering not quite ready to take leave of the festival.

I showed you the end of the rope, poking it out from under my coat. I took your hand and had you feel it. You smiled. I couldn't see your face, but I could sense your smile. On our bellies, we crawled past the dead line into the ditch and up the other side, pressing up against the wooden beams of the stockade. We breathed deeply. I looked around. Everything was quiet. We could hear one of the sentries singing Dixie softly to himself from a nearby tower. I took out the rope and began to let out the coils. I counted about four arm spans and tied up the end in a knot with a rock. Then I took two steps back with the rope in both hands and waited until the song reached the chorus, "away, away," and let fly. There was a slight muffled knock as the knot caught in the notch between beams. I pulled a couple of hauls to make sure it was set tight. The singer in the distant tower concluded his piece, and there were hand claps and whistles from some of his neighbors.

'You go first,' I whispered to you.

'Why?'

'You're the lighter man.'

You smiled. And then began your ascent, pulling yourself up one hand hold at a time, swiftly and surely. At the top, I watched as you hauled yourself over, and I waited. Then you fell, with a solid thump, on the ground. There was dead silence, just the wind whistling and moaning. I heard a knock on the wall. I shivered, fearing the worst, despite the signal that you were alive and well. I knocked back.

I began my climb, not at all sure of success. It's true that desperation lends a helping hand when mental fibers prove as strong or stronger than mere muscle. Near the top I heard the linen tear and lunged for the final yard, my hand just clearing the last inch of rough, sharpened wood. With the last reserves of will, I pulled myself up and my legs angled over. Not strong enough to hang and steady myself at the top, not sure if I was on the right side or not, I fell, and the time stretched for what seemed a period intended for me to reason and berate myself for not being able to straighten out, for failing in minor ways when the main battle had been fought. I lost consciousness on impact with the ground. When I came to, you had my head in your lap.

'Am I alive, Joe?'

'You took a bad fall,' you whispered. 'Can you stand?'

'I'll try,' I said.

'Let's move,' you said.

With your help, I was able to shuffle along until my head cleared. I had bruised my side, and it was difficult to breathe. But we made it into the woods. Sighting by the North Star the way father liked to do on late winter nights in Hopkinton as we put out buckets on the maple trees, we came out on the far side of that thicket. There was a long, straight road heading past several large farms. Dogs barked, alerting the families living inside.

We took two draft horses from the barn, creaking it open and riding out bareback along the road. Voices proclaimed loudly in our wake. We disregarded the shouts of outrage and spurred them horses into a gallop. When we reached the outskirts of a town we dismounted and let them go into a field.

We knocked on the door of the nearest house. It looked like it belonged to a craftsman of some kind, tools lying around in the front yard and scraps of wood. A young woman answered in her nightgown, two children poking their heads out from behind her. In the candle light, we could see her husband in a chair, seated, unable to rise. He was an invalid, and we surmised that he labored as a wheelwright by the quantity of knobs and spokes of all sizes and boxes of iron bolts lined up in shelves along the walls.

'Evening, ma'am,' I said, speaking for us both. 'Thank you for your hospitality.'

'What do you men want from us? We are humble and right living believers. We'll do what we can to help y'all,' she said.

'Well, that's good to know, surely. Ma'am, we're just scouts with General Kilpatrick's cavalry. We've been riding for days. That's why our appearance is so wild and uncivilized, like. I can imagine you folks are afeard, but I can assure you and your kin there's no reason for it. This is a nice house and you are nice, good people, we can tell. Can you spare a change of clothes and some

victuals? We'll be on our way and you'll be put down as the helping kind that will see no harm come to you.'

'Where's the rest of your company?' asked the man seated in his chair, in the dark. His voice was strong, but his legs were useless.

'The troops have set up camp to the west of us here, sir. We're on our way to Macon, and I think there's no Rebel boys putting up much of a fight in this part of the country,' you said.

'That's because Lee has sent them to defend Savannah,' the woman responded gamely.

'That may well be,' I answered. 'Our orders are to scout for food and the sentiments of the people along the way.'

'We don't have much in the way of food, but you can have what little we can spare. And as for a change of clothes, Martin here has some britches and a shirt or two he can give you.'

'That would be most kind of you, ma'am,' I said. 'This here will do for our horses,' I pointed to a bushel basket of apples on a side table.

The woman, whose name was May, set out some hard bread and cottage cheese. We ate what we could stuff down and changed right there in front of the stunned family into Martin's britches and shirts under our coats and put back on our boots and our caps back on our heads. Our dirty Union uniforms we left in a pile by the door. I suspect they probably burned them right away. I carried the basket of apples, and you led the way back across the road to the field where the horses grazed, outlined in the starlight. I took leave in the doorway and thanked the family again for their support, assuring May of our gratitude and of her and Martin and their two boys' security for the duration of hostilities between the warring factions of our unsettled country.

When we got to Macon, we had ridden through the night. Abandoning the horses again in some middling ground on the outskirts, we made our way by foot into the center. It had been a long strange ride, and the two of us were changed forever by it. No longer just brothers, joined by custom and blood, we had become co-conspirators in some pageant that had been devised long before our coming. At the train station, you stopped.

'I'm not coming home with you, Bill.'

'Why the hell not?'

'Just something's come over me. I don't know what it is, but these are strange times. I must obey what I hear.'

'What is it you hear exactly?' I asked, somewhat exasperated. But I'd learned to trust in you, despite your impossible way of making your path in the wilderness.

'I don't know exactly, but it's a voice like a big sky, a summer sky when you're done haying and, and you lie down and look up and the clouds are spinning. Your head is like a top but your heart is good. Know what I mean, Bill?'

'Not exactly.'

'I've gotta chase that feeling. It's not at home in Hopkinton anymore. Mother can take care of herself and so can you now. You

ride that train back north and leave me to follow my voice. When I find it, I'll let you know. I'll write home and let you know.'

It was hard for me to let you go after that night ride. I was forever changed, and I knew you were also.

'I'll pray you find whatever it is you're looking for. As for me...' I said with difficulty.

'I know, Bill. I know. The farm, a picket fence.'

'Jane Forrest.'

'She still loves you.'

'Roast chestnuts by the fire.'

'You go find Jane and roast you some big pile of chestnuts, Bill,' you said.

That was the last time we spoke. But life went on. I imagine you crossing many rivers on the way to your haying field. And a voice guiding you, a big voice from on high somewhere, sounding a horn of victory.

The room had a small bed, a sink, and a light on a side table. The light was on. There were no windows. Sid stood from the bed. He could hear the propane furnace pumping heat through the copper pipes that went around the basement over his head. The bricks were painted white. He put on sweatpants and a fresh shirt that was folded on top of the hamper by the door. He splashed water on his face and slicked back his hair and dried off with the green terry cloth bathrobe hanging on a hook on the wall. There was a painting, a pencil sketch drawing of a clipper boat docked at a busy harbor, masts of schooners filling the space to the horizon, on the white brick wall.

Sid opened the door and stepped into the rest of the basement. He looked through the small window that poked out above ground. He couldn't see the tires. The little man was gone. He walked upstairs. The Persian carpets on the living room floor were worn. The bookcases were full of academic studies on public health and classics in the fields of economics, contemporary literature, and philosophy. There were faded, framed photographs set among the books on the wide bookshelves of the man in younger days side by side a handsome, broad woman with neatly presented dark hair, both of them smiling confidently. Somewhere, Sid could hear voices approaching. As he stood there on the living room floor, a door on the opposite side of the room opened. It was Marta, the housekeeper. She smiled at Sid. She was wearing jeans and a smock and carrying a vacuum cleaner in one hand, dragging it through the door.

"You want some breakfast? Jordan and Patrick already eat."

"No. That's okay. I'll eat in a while," said Sid. The cereal and cold scrambled eggs would still be out on the table.

"Oh, okay," said Marta. Sid inspected her figure as she plugged the cord into the wall outlet under the mullioned window.

"When did she die?"

"Who die?"

"The wife."

“Oh. Mrs. Schwartz. About I don’t know, seven, eight years ago, I guess.”

“Did you know her?”

“Yes. She was a wonderful woman. Jordan miss her a lot. They love each other. So cute. Rided bicycles all the time here, Europe, all over. It was sad. Very sad when she die.”

She started the vacuum. Sid continued on his way past her, stepping gingerly across the path of the vacuum head. Marta smiled coyly. Sid had a small jolt of adrenaline hit the back of his head. He realized this was the subconscious mind reaching out to him with some of his old, bad habits. He was a twisted bit of the subconscious mind of the planet that for some reason, probably having to do with 19 years of incarceration in the correctional facility, had torqued beyond repair. There was no reason. All these reasonable efforts led back to the rise and fall of creatures out of the swamp. They rose and fell, and their offspring for a time, for a limited time, stood clear and free, able to breathe and convince themselves that this was indeed an intentional consequence of the good graces that swept in on a solar wind.

Patrick was at the table with his feet splayed out sideways into the dining room. The light from the bay window shone brightly on the orderly table with coffee pot, milk jug, bowls and plates in their proper settings and boxes of mostly healthy, organic cereals arranged in the middle. There were also a couple of cold slices of multigrain toast still left in a basket along with a half stick of butter and a small jar of Stonewall Kitchen grape jelly on small plates.

"There they go," said Patrick.

A couple of bicycles whizzed by in the street. They were wearing masks. This occupied Patrick's attention briefly. He was on his phone.

"What the heck? Forty five new cases in Massachusetts? Why don't they lock it down now? Right now?"

"Lock it down. Good idea," said Sid, guiltily recalling what the words had meant just a few short weeks ago. Here he was, a free man but panic stricken. He buttered a slice of the cold toast and shoved it in his mouth as fast as he could. He was actually ravenous.

"Try the jelly. It's very good," said Patrick. "How's your immune response, Sid?" he asked.

Sid sat down at the table in front of a place setting and buttered another slice. He opened the jar of jelly before thinking of an appropriate answer.

"It's usually good. But it's only as good as you think."

"That's right. You don't know what you don't know, right?" said Patrick.

"Yeah."

"And Sid, this is an unprecedented situation. Different from any other. Notice I didn't say different than. It's different from."

"Yeah," agreed Sid. He poured some of the still warm coffee and sipped it, wiping his mouth with the sleeve of his flannel shirt.

"You know, it looks like you're going to be here for a few weeks at least. You might as well relax and enjoy your stay here, man," said Patrick.

"I don't know," said Sid.

"Try the jelly."

"I am."

Patrick stared hard at the butter knife that Sid wielded on the last slice of cold toast. He was hyper focused, in fact. It made Sid really uncomfortable. But then he went back to his phone. Sid studied the jar of grape jelly, reading the ingredients, instead of actually using it on the toast. He ate in peace and drank the coffee. It was a civilized affair, these late morning breakfasts in Jordan's house in Boston. He had no idea what time or day it was. He'd been there perhaps three days. He remembered the little man on the curb of Massachusetts Avenue that night on his phone. With Marta on one arm and the little man on the other, Sid had entered the car and away from the street he had gone, to become instead a novel part of Jordan's experiment in private philanthropy.

"Did you have a good session this morning, Patrick?" he asked.

"Oh. Yeah. Very good. I'm feeling that much closer to being a good person, Sid. My paranoia, hypochondria and general misery are in full retreat. The world is a wonderful place. Is it not?"

"I don't think it's so bad."

"Well you're just being a fucking wuss. Stop the passive-aggressive, amiable giant act, Sid. Ever heard of the Corona virus? We're fucked."

Sid smiled and chewed. Patrick reminded him of the theater geeks in high school who modeled themselves on Prince and Edie

Brickell. He meant well, but was chronically depressed, in fact suicidal. He had been, not long ago, a Tufts graduate student, and before that, a black kid from a middle class home in the suburbs north of New York. He had dropped out of Tufts and taken to the street in Somerville, where Jordan had found him in the summer, raving outside a burger joint about T.S. Eliott and rats and peasants and the phones being tapped. He still had the same phone, with its cracked screen and zero service. He now recognized it probably wasn't being tapped, at least aside from the way the entire world's phone service was jacked and categorized for dubious connections.

Sid was lying in bed when Jordan knocked on the door.

"Can I come in, Sid?"

"Sure," said Sid, staring at the ceiling.

Jordan Schwartz's forehead was covered in liver spots. His hands sported large varicose veins. He was so ugly it was fascinating to watch his face. Sid tried to glean something from his hooded eyes. When Jordan looked up, there was a slight smile playing in his pupils, a recognition that he was oddly attractive. It was a tremendous advantage in getting his way. Sid was sure he regularly, or had at one point anyway, slept with Marta. Jordan settled himself on the stool he always brought in with him, so that he was barely above Sid's eye level when he sat. Sid scooched up with his back under a pillow so that he could see the little man better.

"No, stay where you are, Sid, stay where you are. I want you to be comfortable."

"I am comfortable. I want to be able to see you."

"Okay. Now, Sid. You're going to relax. Remember to breathe deeply in and out. Feel your toes. How's your feet doing?"

"Better."

"Bare feet. As soon as it gets warmer we'll take you out to the beach. Imagine you're walking in the warm sand barefoot, Sid. On the beach. In the summer. The breeze is warm, blowing in your face, there's the sweet salt smell, some seagulls flying. You breathe deeply. The waves are coming in. You're watching the waves as they come in, long lines of waves coming onto the beach and the sound of the surf and the seagulls flying. There's also kites flying in the wind, and children and dogs playing and you're walking along the sand. Feel your toes digging in the warm sand, moving your body easily down the beach. You're not in any hurry. You're enjoying the sun on your skin, the warm breeze. There's so much going on but you just let it all wash over you. You're just a part of the day, a part of life on the beach. You're no better or worse. Everybody is on the beach together. There's children playing. Dogs playing. Seagulls flying. The smell of the salt and the sounds of the wind and people just there on the beach with you. There's no shame, no envy. You're just glad to be alive. You're walking along. Your bare feet are strong. There's no pain. You breathe deeply. Get that salt air in your lungs, filling them with fresh air. Such fresh air. Feel the warm sand spreading your toes. The millions of grains of sand beneath your feet, your toes digging through the sand. That sand that's taken millions of years to form. Rocks breaking down, crumbling into grains from millions of years of waves, and sun, and wind. The long lines of waves crashing on the beach, endlessly. Forever."

Jordan's voice droned on while Sid slipped into a dream. He saw himself in the chicken house in Loonberg. The chickens jumped and pecked at his legs as he stood there with the can of feed. His toes were practically bursting through the moldy sneakers, he was growing so fast. The chickens pecked at the sneakers. He wanted to let them have the can of feed, but he couldn't resist teasing them, holding back to make them anxious. He tried looking them in their little, red, unblinking eyes. They seemed distraught constantly, and would not calm down even with the food from the can. Sid understood as a child the power of the one who holds the can of food. In the hierarchy of the chickens of the dream, Sid was the crazy god who sometimes showed up on time and sometimes forgot.

Jordan asked him how he was feeling now.

"Better," said Sid.

"Yeah. That's good," said Jordan cheerily.

"What's the point of the rocks breaking down, Jordan? All that energy and motion breaking down the rocks. Is there a point?"

"I like that you're reflecting on the journey, Sid. What's the point? Maybe nothing is permanent. Maybe we shouldn't hold on to things so much. We should go with the flow, the process, if you like. It's the way of the universe. You know, like the Tao says, the great Chinese tradition of the Tao, which developed a doctrine, a methodology to help people deal with life. It said we should mold ourselves to the path of Nature and try to emulate what we can observe from the natural world. I feel like you're someone who's observed the natural world and has tried to develop your own lessons, Sid. But sometimes those lessons that we've held onto since childhood, they can lead us into the backwoods. The wilderness. Know what I mean?"

"Yeah," said Sid, agreeing. But Sid still felt like there was a flaw to all Jordan's philanthropic impulses. Not his methods. Listening to Jordan and relaxing into the state of mind of receptivity and relaxed attention definitely helped to clear his muddled thoughts and self-destructive desires, and it had been a few days since he'd craved something, some miracle to ingest, some silver bullet to take his mind off the pains in his feet and the aches of his heart.

"What does God want from us, though, Jordan? I mean like chickens lay eggs. What are we supposed to be doing to make us whole in the eyes of God?"

"I don't think you need to bring God into it, Sid."

"But you can."

"Yes. Sure. You can. But you don't have to."

"Maybe you do, though. What if you do?"

Jordan stared at his hands as they massaged each other.

"I had an uncle, Sid, who survived the Chelmno extermination camp."

"What was his name?"

"His name? Maurice."

"Maurice what?"

"Maurice Margolis. I don't know if they had last names in Russia. But they were the Margolises when they got to America. Anyway, he was the last uncle to make it. After the war. In 1952 he gets to Philadelphia. He used to tell me stories. He taught me how to do card tricks to calm me down when I was a just a little boy. Sid, I asked him about God, figuring he knew a thing or two having survived the Chelmno camp, one of the worst, by the way, that the Nazis devised. I'll tell you about it someday. But I said, 'Uncle Maurice, is there God? Is He watching all of this?'"

"Yeah, exactly," said Sid.

"Right. Do you know what he said? I remember to this day, Sid. He goes 'Why does God always have to move in mysterious ways? I could believe in him better if he took the time to explain what his intentions were.' Or something like that. Look, maybe there is a God, but he clearly doesn't speak our language. What's the point if we don't have a key that could explain his thinking? And don't tell me the Bible. The Bible explains whatever you want it to. You could believe in anything or nothing and it would be the same in the end, Sid. All it does, this religious cast, is lead to manic depression and maybe worse. Social isolation. Just you and God in some form of communion that usually involves intense suffering."

"Maybe that's the point."

"No. That's exactly, precisely not the point. Am I your friend, Sid? Would you say?"

"Well, of course you are, Jordan."

"Our oath as friends, Sid, never mind fathers and brothers and sons and daughters, is to reduce suffering. Suffering is the enemy of mankind and always will be. Suffering is not the point. In that way lies madness."

"Yeah," said Sid. "I don't know. Maybe."

"We need to be useful to each other."

Sid swung his feet and stood from the foot of the bed. He paced in the small room. Jordan watched him, unnerved by the large swing of movement, fragile seeming as he slumped on the stool, and Sid wrestled with the weight of his thoughts, paying little attention to the little man.

The fence posts in the backyard of Jordan's house were recently painted. The posts were fine-grained and smooth to the touch. Sid did not know what sort of wood they were. Not softwood. Some sort of fancy plastic, he guessed. Treated. The miracles of chemistry. Fence posts like this did not exist north of Worcester. On the other side a dog barked. It was mid-morning and cloudy. Sid thought of Rover. In his mind also were all the people whom he missed: Ruth, Leesha, Lesli. A siren sounded. The hospital was just a few blocks away. They were in lockdown mode called by the Commonwealth of Massachusetts. Nonessential services were closed. Jordan no longer went out much except in the mornings, very early. Marta had been doing the shopping on her way into work from her home in Melrose, but now she was there to stay. She had abandoned her home, where she lived alone anyway, to care for her master and his charges. It was all very Biblical, Sid thought. It was ironic, given Jordan's clear anti-church stance. It was as if Jordan was trapped in a web that he had failed to perceive. They all were.

He'd been in Jordan's house now for a couple of weeks. Patrick had stayed once before for three years, according to Marta. In his teens, he'd been a tennis star in high school as well as a theater geek, until he got into huffing Ritalin. Later crack cocaine. He and Patrick had gotten high on legal marijuana that Jordan kept in a stash in the dining room on one of the bookshelves. It was intended for anybody's use. Jordan was not averse to drug use. In a limited way it could be helpful, or at least not as harmful as portrayed. Sid felt that was a double-edged sword. Every time he got high he heard voices and hallucinated that he was being watched by mercenary forces with undisclosed intentions. What those intentions were was a mystery. But Sid never got the impression that they were benevolent. Maybe that was his paranoia, doubting the motivations of his imaginary pursuers. Maybe they had his best interests at heart. Maybe they knew things he didn't. He had an unclear handle on things at best. Getting high made it clear that there was tremendous uncertainty at all times and historical periods. But in the end, given the uncertainty of everything, Sid trusted the voices that he heard in dreams. They told him to run early and fast, and so he did. He trusted nobody. His feet hurt. His heart ached. Some things did not change. Jesus wept. It was Easter. There were no church bells ringing and had not been for many years.

Case numbers had climbed precipitously. Nobody had expected the way they increased overnight. It seemed eerily like a horror movie. The streets had emptied, as Sid could attest. He watched through the little basement window. Jordan still went out in the mornings in his car. He wore an N-95 mask. Sid could see, if he peered up at the right angle as Jordan walked out to the car. He did rounds at the hospital as a volunteer. He didn't want to talk about it. His concern for their well-being, the creatures under his care, Sid and Patrick, was increasingly professional and under a strain. Jordan always needed fresh patients to feel like he made a difference in the large picture, the overall frame, but the homeless had been cleared from the streets by orders from on high. Jordan felt useless. His expertise as an alternative practitioner was of little value in the hospital in the pandemic. Orthodoxy reigned supreme. The experts weighed in. Jordan mumbled rebelliously as he ate with them at night, about the choices being made in the name of everyone's good. It was worse than the disease, Jordan thought.

Sid thought that the world was bending in the direction it was slanted anyway, long before the virus swept in from wherever. Marta never went home. She had a room on the first floor, a converted spare room that had been a storage room for bicycles and workout equipment that had belonged to Jordan's wife. One day, he was in there. It was evening. The television was on. He was lying on the bed next to Marta. They were both dressed, but barefoot. Her toes were twisted and mangled, worse than his. Her feet were small, stumplike. It was a wonder that she could walk at all. The news was on. The deaths were climbing. The hospitals were putting a brave face on the lack of supplies. The nation was losing. It was another lost cause. It made Sid feel glad he had no part in it. Marta was nice to him.

"I'm scared, Sid," she said.

"Why?" asked Sid.

"The Corona. If I get it, that's bad for my family in the Philippines."

"Why?"

"I send them money they use for rent, food, school, everything. My family, Sid."

"What about your son? Where is he? Gloucester?"

"He's okay. He's a strong boy. He's living I guess in Salem. But me, my lungs not too good. I used to smoke."

"Yeah," said Sid.

"Can you kiss me, Sid? Make me feel better?"

Sid turned his head. Marta was looking at him with a half wistful, half wild expression.

"I can't, Marta."

"Why the hell not, Sid?"

"I might hurt you. I wouldn't want to do that. You're too good to me."

"Ah, okay," said Marta.

She said it as though something had clarified for her. Sid wondered what Marta was thinking about. He looked at her and she was now sort of smiling at something without looking directly at him. She had a mole underneath her right eye.

"What are you thinking, Marta?" asked Sid.

"You need to find you mother, Sid. Talk to her. She did something, make you think bad is good. You can only love someone who's cruel. That's wrong, Sid. That's fucked up. Someone who's good to you, who take care of you, they deserve you love, Sid. You don't have to hurt nobody. You just a big, fucked up guy. Typical shit, Sid. Nothing wrong with you."

"You think it's my mother?"

"Somebody."

"She's dead."

"Are you sure? I believe she alive, Sid. You wouldn't still be hurting so bad if she dead. She be looking out for you better."

Sid felt that the cloud was lifting. He was sleeping decently for the first time in his life. He was eating solid food for breakfast. After breakfast he would have long talks with Jordan in which he revealed himself and then afterwards did not care if what was revealed no longer seemed true or tenable in any way. He was bored. But his boredom was a manifestation of a state of mind he'd never associated with before, a condition of privilege. Jordan's bookshelves in the dining room spilled over into the living room area. Patrick would be usually silent, cuddled into himself on a sofa, reading something on his phone. Sid would pull down books and read long passages, forcing himself to skim the words and then repeat until he had accumulated emotional content from these. He savored his responses and then was disgusted with himself and all the words in the books. Some of the titles he pulled down were: *The Origins of Totalitarianism, Slaughterhouse Five, On Earth We're*

Briefly Gorgeous, Capital and Ideology. There was something that compelled him, despite his initial feelings of disgust with these imperious books and the emptiness their litany of strange words engendered. When he read, he would drain all the toxins from his gut. It was like taking a bowel movement. And then he was left with dull echoes that might set off resonances within him, he hoped. He dearly hoped.

"Seven thousand cases, Sid. A hundred twenty two motherfucking dead," said Patrick one day.

"Keep going, Patrick.What are we going to do?"

"We only have two choices."

"What's that?"

"Hope it goes away or go out and face it. It's just fear at this point that's beating us down. We're not fearful people, Sid. We're not built that way. We can't let it become the new normal."

"I agree," said Sid.

"Gotta remember the Chief. What did Chief Bromden say, Sid? Do you remember?"

"No," said Sid sadly.

"He said: '*But it's the truth, even if it didn't happen.*' That's the motherfucking way," said Patrick.

"Yeah, maybe," said Sid.

"Take on reality itself in the name of the truth. See, everybody thought the Chief was deaf and dumb, Sid, but he was a fearless warrior. Like you."

“Thank you, Patrick. I like to think so. You gotta choose your battles, though, Patrick,” said Sid.

“Yeah, but sometimes they choose you.”

It might have been that very night that Patrick decided to take his life. He used a belt and fashioned a makeshift noose. He hung himself from a hook above the closet door on the third floor of Jordan’s house. He died at some point in the early part of the night, but was not discovered by Marta until the next morning. She knocked several times, and when there was no response she barged in. At that moment Sid was lifting a spoon to his mouth at the dining room table. He heard a loud clunk. It was Marta’s body, her shoulder and skull hitting the hardwood floor of the bedroom above him.

EMTs in surgical masks and plastic hair nets lifted Patrick’s body onto the stretcher and covered his face with the sheet. Sid watched with Marta from the foyer as they went out the door. Marta nursed herself with a bag of frozen peas held to her forehead. The ambulance was parked on the street in front of the house. Passersby practicing the proper social distance turned their heads, crossed the street, and slouched forward on their way faster. Jordan sat on the sofa with his little legs splayed apart and a highball glass half filled in his lap. He had shrunk into himself. The ambulance turned on its siren for a split second to ease its way into the non-existent traffic. The street was empty. The door was still open. Sid walked out and stretched. He looked back at the house. He could follow the ambulance and make his way somewhere new. But he was careful now in new ways. He feared leaving. He realized that Patrick’s death was meant to sever such bonds. In a way, Patrick intended to cut them all loose, but he had only succeeded in causing them to grip the handles of the knives tighter than before. Sid was barefoot. He went back into the house and found his boots in the basement. He pulled them on, fastening them with a new found appreciation for the way they were meant to protect his feet from the elements. The Beothuk had sewn moccasins from the tanned hide of deer and caribou. In this way they had made their way as the ice melted behind them.

Sid went back upstairs. There were birds chirping in the street, among the trees that were beginning to bud out new leaves.

"I'm leaving," he told Marta and Jordan. Jordan turned his head from the sofa and looked at him in an expression that combined disbelief and disdain. Marta was crying in silent tears that ran down her face. She seemed dignified but broken by Patrick's death. She came up to him and held out her arms. Sid bent low and hugged her and felt her hot tears on his face. He smiled at her.

"Don't be sad for me, Marta," he said.

"It's you time, Sid. Just be careful out there," said Marta.

"You know where you're going, Sid?" asked Jordan.

"No," said Sid.

"Wear a mask. You really need a mask," said Jordan.

Sid held up his arm and crooked his head into the elbow. He turned and went to the door. Nobody greeted him on the street. Holding his arm up to cover his face, Sid ventured forth into the city.

VI. The Plague City

Sid listened to the voices that guided him spontaneously down the radiating streets, branching like aureoles. They alternately warned and encouraged, chilled and heated, and Sid proceeded in a fever pitch, taking corners, looping around reservoirs and housing developments. There were few cars out. Buses were still running, but paid him no heed. They had nothing to do with him. Sid was in a different city, the plague city, the dead piling up in the alleyways and the secret parking lots of refrigerated trucks on the outskirts. The dead congested the arteries of the secret city. Crying children and the sound of smashing plates were a constant drone. A pickup truck full of ladders slowed and studied him. The driver leaned over and looked him in the eye. Instantly, the driver understood that Sid was a pilgrim on a separate orbit, following a star that had appeared, but was not visible overhead. His star was guiding him, though, which was more than you could say of the rest of the place in those days, rudderless, without a compass, suddenly lost and drowning in mixed signals and dystopic administrations. The driver left Sid and carried on with his duty, diligently, the better for having seen the mad look in Sid's eyes. It gave him faith that salvation was at hand, for Sid was like a prophet with understanding at last after years of hunger and associated tribulations, while the good children were stunned and missed the tinkling of bells that usually preceded their meals.

Sid was not alone. Hordes of angels and demons followed in his wake. Where he planted his feet sprung up geysers of steam. Sid followed the path of underground streams, sensing the weight of geological striations with his feet, attuned to the lay of time. Asphalt and brick gave way to marl and silt. Sid's head cleaved the air. Then he saw as if from on high that the city was on a rock above the raging storm. There was no need to fear destruction. The rock was solid, an outcropping of the original spume cast from the sea by the creator's first wild impulse. It was built on the foundation of the timeless mind and held in place by the oaths of all the supernumeraries. Sid walked among the angels and demons, turning to them to say that at last he understood what they had been going through. Patrick was there. He could see him on the bus that never stopped. It just went on and on with all the people bound for the terminal, the South Station of the Intergalactic Web. It stretched in Sid's mind, and he saw that Patrick was right. There was no need for fear. Fear was an invention of the sick to keep the healthy from over-running the planet. Fear was a virus that had mutated in its passage from the wet markets of China. Fear was good. It kept the healthy from instituting measures to guarantee their sons and daughters took everything. The sons and daughters of the healthy were nowhere to be seen. They were indoors, with the computers on. Out on the street with Sid were the angels and the demons. And the buses never stopped. There was no fear on these buses. Nobody was wearing masks or practicing the safe measures. There were no computers on. Sid thought about computers. Everything was in them. Every secret conversation and every manifestation of the imminent could be discovered if you had the key. Jordan had talked about the key. It was there in the computers. Man had a tool to converse with the infinite that dwelled within. But for Sid the way of the Beothuk beckoned with greater strength and majesty. Find your way to the edge of the land. Make the dawn your own castle. Fortify yourself against your enemies, and when they arrive, fight with all your power, will, strength, and guile, and go into your certain death without fear. Then years later your descendants will honor you. They will ride the buses and walk the streets like heroes, while the children of the healthy cower indoors against the sickness, helpless, counting their silverware and the length of the peaks, the light fading in their glass towers.

Sid looked in through the shuttered gate at the wares of Dream Parts, cell phones and laptops and for some reason green plastic Christmas tree stands. Someone came up behind him.

"Doesn't look like it's open," said a teenage girl, about seventeen. She stood on the curb, her face half covered in a bandanna.

"I could see the point if there was a key," said Sid.

"You don't have the key," said the girl. "It's not open, in case you hadn't noticed."

"The key will set you free," said Sid.

"I could use a new Iphone, though," said the girl. "Whatever it is you're thinking, you want a heck of a sledgehammer to smash those shutters. Plus the police come through here about five times a day."

"What's the point, though? It's poisoning your brain, my brain. All our brains. We're all infected. The cure is worse than the disease."

"Okay. You sound like my grandfather. Look, technology is a tool. You want to jack the system, you need the right tools. But first you're going to need a sledgehammer to get through those shutters. So if I were you I'd quit dreaming and get a fucking big hammer."

Sid looked at the girl. She seemed to be a manifestation of a subterranean voice that had no use other than opening up the portals of his awareness to the possibilities in chaos. She was confused and covering her ass, the worst combination of denial and pride he could think of. He couldn't see her mouth behind the bandanna, but he was sure she was smirking by the light of her eyes.

"Don't waste your time, kid," he said. But she was gone.

Sid observed the street from the Dream Parts store. The southern side of the street was in shadow. Sid was feeling hidden by the darkness. On the other side, the northern side, pedestrians stripped down. A couple of children in tee shirts skated by. The voices rose and fell. Sid tried not to talk to himself. It was a discipline, but it didn't really help. He tried not to read the minds of people in passing cars. That was a flagrant abuse of the rules of domesticity, of living with others, that he had learned in the correctional facility. “Shut the fuck up,” he said to himself, when a thought popped up that was unwarranted.

Why did his mind do that? Why did he think he had access to some telepathic current that allowed him precious insight into his fellows, not in some abstract sense, but directly and intuitively, like a wild animal had use of the forest, posted against trespass. In the correctional facility, you would get challenged openly once you started down that road. Some little turd would see it immediately in your face, your eyes, and your helplessly twitching body because you wanted to be found out. That was part of your body’s secret plan to overthrow your mind. The tyrannical mind that had chosen that route of escape, and it meant you were no longer living by the rules of domesticity and collaboration but had chosen to put yourself above your fellows as judge and ruler of the sphere that was not only your own private sphere but one that included the thoughts and feelings of the others. And your body with its subversive, proletarian tricks it had learned when you weren’t even paying attention yet. Some little guy, some striker would step up in the yard and wave you on, and the quick circle would form. Before you knew it there would be blood, and one of you would shoot for the body and down to the ground and then the shouting as elbows and fists flew spasmodically, and the guards, guys with big bellies and wives and lives on the outside, would break it up, pulling at wrists and choking you with head-holds. But not before solidarity had been reset. Sid missed all of that. He missed human beings and the messy ties that bound them all together and the unspoken rules of conflict and resolution. Out here on Commonwealth Avenue there were just these shuttered dreams. Sid waited for heaven to open. He could be as patient as Ali Baba's thieves.

The girl reappeared. The bandanna was different. She had a plastic bag of food in one hand, takeout, and the phone in the other. The takeout bag steamed with delicious smells. She was trying out a different look with the bandanna stretched on her face. She took a picture of Sid sitting on the steps with her phone and went up the street. When she came back, she was talking on the phone, holding it down by her side. The metallic voice on the other end droned on and stopped, aware of her indifference.

"Paula? Are you there?"

"Yes. He's still here. I want you to call somebody. There's tents set up on Southampton Street, Daddy. I know they're using dorms at Suffolk University, too."

"Calm down. Come back inside and eat. Mama's hungry and so am I. Did you get the sashimi?"

"I have it here," she said as she stepped by Sid. He scooted over on the brick step. The metallic voice droned on behind him and the big door swung shut. Minutes later it opened again. Sid did not turn around. He'd been expecting this.

"Hey you, guy. You, ah, can't sit there. Just loitering like that. We're gonna have to call the police. D'ya hear me?"

"You always were a little too tight-assed for my taste," said Sid.

The man stepped by him onto the sidewalk with an impatient lilt to his cadence.

Sid stayed put. His back hunched over a little further, just slightly. But this time there was no betrayal. It was a telegraphed move on purpose. He didn’t look up, but instead studied the cracks in the pavement between his feet.

“What did you say?” asked the man.

“You were always a little bit shitty, and it doesn't surprise me in the least to see you like this now, Darrell. You have nobody but yourself to thank for any of this.” Sid spoke into the ground, mumbling his words.

“Sid?”

The man adjusted his mask, stepped forward. He got down on his knees to peer into Sid’s face.

“Sid,” he said again.

“I found you,” said Sid. “I told you I would. Did you think you could hide from me, little brother?”

Angela, Darrell’s wife and the mother of the aggressively posed teenager, was not happy. She made it plain with deeply downturned lips and quick mouth clicks at any suggestion Darrel made to reclaim peace in his house. Sid thought it best to stay silent. He was seated at Darrell’s side at the marble-topped counter where they gathered on Nordic bar stools for meals. Angela had a scarf of tropical colors on her head and a sweatshirt that said Mt. Agnes College.

"Darrell, this is an outrage that cannot stand. It is not sustainable, *mi amor*. Where do you suppose we can go now? Wash your hands? *Ay, coño.* Not enough soap. Not enough toilet paper. Where do you think you're going, young lady?"

"Out," said Paula.

"You can't do that. It's against the law," bleated Angela. But she was ignored.

Paula stood. She found her bandanna in her pocket, stretched it over her mouth, and left the apartment, pulling the door violently shut. But it seemed to have some sort of braking mechanism that prevented it from slamming. This was the sort of gadget Darrel and Sid could only have imagined back in the New Hampshire woods. It was the civilized touches that set him apart, immune from the diseases of the rest of unwashed humanity.

Darrell had his forehead in his hands. The plate of arepas had been pushed to the center of the island. Sid took one and stuffed it with cheese before popping it in his mouth. Angela glared at him. Darrell looked up.

"What's wrong with the soap?" asked Darrell.

"You bought the wrong kind. Who uses Ivory? My God," said Angela.

"That's what kind we used to use. Right, Sid?"

"That's right. Ivory soap. Wash your mouth out with it," mumbled Sid.

"That was Yolanda. She was strict," said Darrell.

"Look. He probably has it already. Look at him," said Angela.

"Come on, Sid. We'll set you up in the study," said Darrell.

"This is not sustainable. You understand?" said Angela.

"It will be fine. What else are we going to do?" asked Darrell.

"*Yo no sé. ¿Qué sé yo?*" asked Angela.

Darrell scooted the bar stool back somehow, pushing off the island with his knees. It screeched on the bamboo floor tiles.

"Come on, Sid. Follow me," he said.

Sid did as he was told. He was impressed by Darrell's apparent ease scooching among the furniture and the turmoil of years. As a self-made man, he seemed to have ditched the baggage that they both had inherited.

In his study, Darrell had a framed photograph on the shelf of the Ferncroft football team a couple of years after Sid had gone into the correctional facility. He recognized a few of the players, including Darrell, who was an end, and of course the coaches, Mr. Hebert the driving instructor and Alfie Cancuso, who used to go to Florida every winter, he remembered.

"Did you guys have a good team?" asked Sid.

"I think we did. We beat Plymouth on senior night. That's all I remember."

"That was a big deal," said Sid.

"Yeah, it was," said Darrell.

Darrell made a bed on the chaise longue by folding a sheet around it and covering it with a blanket. He placed a folded towel at the foot of it.

"There you go, Sid," said Darrell. He sat on the chaise longue. Sid sat in the swivel office chair and swiveled a little just to stretch his legs. He realized that Darrell was crying.

"Thank you Darrell. You didn't have to do this," he said.

"I know it's hard for you, Sid."

"Are we the same people we were, Darrell?"

"You gotta ask?"

Darrell sniffled and wiped his face with his palm.

"You want to take a shower?" he asked.

"I'm good," said Sid.

"How's your health? Did they take care of that at least?"

"Pretty good. I had a couple of checkups through the years. I think my cholesterol is a little high and my blood pressure is too. But other than my head, I'm pretty solid, buddy," said Sid.

"Good," said Darrell. "I mean your head was always a little hard. That hasn't changed, I guess."

"Softened up a bit, buddy," said Sid, laughing. This was good for him, seeing his brother, but Sid sensed that the gulf between them that had opened up over the years was insurmountable, despite Darrel's tears.

"You look good," said Sid, trying half-heartedly to keep the conversation going.

"I cycle," said Darrell.

"You cycle?" asked Sid.

"Yeah. I've got an alloy road bike with carbon forks. Seven thousand bucks."

"Can I borrow it?"

"No fucking way."

Sid smiled to himself. He coughed. This was more like Darrell.

"You okay?" asked Darrell. "Your face, I can't read it. Your emotions, Sid. Do you think maybe we're missing something that other people take for granted? An ability to read ordinary human emotions?"

"How about feel ordinary human emotions?" said Sid. He felt sensitive suddenly, as if Darrell had dishonored the family name, instead of identifying a key flaw that had gone undiagnosed in both of them. Darrell seemed at a loss for words.

"I think I'll lie down for a while, Darrell," said Sid.

"You can do that. You definitely can do that, Sid. You…" Darrell didn't finish his thought. He went out, closing the study door. It closed almost without a sound. The hinges looked brand new. Everything was new. The carpeting was clean and grey and extended under the door, another insulating layer against pain and discomfort. Sid lay down on the chaise longue and covered his shoulders with the blanket.

By night-time, Sid was coughing all the time. His whole body was in a dull kind of pain that reminded him of the aftermath of

Steve and his beatings. He was curled up fetal on the chaise longue. Darrell and Angela knocked on the door and entered, wearing masks.

"You okay, Sid?" asked Darrell.

"I'm fine. I'll be fine," said Sid.

"We've got you some food here. It's just outside the door," said Darrell.

"Thanks," said Sid, exploding with a cough that bellowed through the door.

Angela and Darrell hurried down the hall, glaring in panic at each other.

Sid sweated through his clothes. He threw the blanket off and rolled over and over, ending up on the floor under the chaise longue, coughing into a corduroy pillow embroidered with the name of the Hilton Head National Golf Club.

In the morning the food was still outside the door. There was no noise. Darrell opened the study door and saw Sid on the chaise longue, shivering. Darrell pulled the mask over his nose.

"How do you feel, Sid? Do you want a doctor?"

"I think I'll be fine. I just need to get warm. I'm freezing.

Darrell walked in and placed the blanket on Sid.

"You didn't eat the food. You didn't like it?"

"I can't eat seafood, Darrell. You know that."

"I'll bring you some more arepa," said Darrell.

"Leave it outside the door," said Sid. Don't come in, Darrell. I think I've got the Corona."

"Yeah, you do," said Darrell.

Sid alternated between heat and cold, his body wracked with the spasms and contortions of an escape artist who had met his match. His mind was storm tossed, sinking for days beneath the water, reflecting submarine dreams, beams of light and dark, columns of color, ancient cities, distant horizons, and sometimes close-ups where the battle raged within the cellular structure of his organs, the hordes of invaders gaining entry here and repulsed there on the fields of his bloodstream and the lining of his respiratory tract. Everywhere was painful. It was hard to breathe. There wasn't any relief. It was impossible to think about anything except breathing. His chest heaved over and over, and Sid thought of a drummer in a marathon dance, listening to himself breathe.

On the fourth day the fever broke. His breathing got easier. Slowly, he came back to full consciousness. Sid opened the door and found a plate of egg salad and fried plantain chips. It was delicious, even the limp iceberg lettuce garnish. He opened the door again and slipped the empty plate onto the carpet. The girl looked at him around the corner. He tried to remember who she was. He closed the door again. She padded down the hall and picked up the plate.

"Are you okay?" she asked, from behind the door.

"Can I have some water?" asked Sid.

"Yeah," she said. He remembered who she was, Darrell's daughter.

She opened the door and walked in, holding out the glass of water. The ice cubes tinkled against the tall glass. Her hand was steady and her look betrayed no emotion.

Sid took the glass.

"What happened to the bandanna?" he asked.

"I'm tired of it," she said.

"You can't be tired of it. It'll save your life," said Sid. He took a long drink of the water and pressed an ice cube between his lips. It felt good. He took a deep breath.

"If we get used to masks, we'll have to wear them forever," she said.

"Why?"

"We'll have to peel them off our skin," she said.

"You're not afraid of dying?" asked Sid.

"No," she said.

"You're a Beothuk. Anybody tell you that?"

"No."

Sid took another deep breath.

"I think I'm going to live," said Sid.

"You've seen a lot, Dad said. It must be tough," said the girl.

What was her name? He couldn't remember. She went out again and closed the door behind her. For two more days, Sid stayed inside. Two days went by. He read the books in Darrell's study. There were only a few. One was *Exceptional Execution: How to Make a Living From Just Your Wits* by Peter Eglin and the other was *A Portrait of My Father* by George Bush. Sid found his mind was calming, solidifying as if the volcanic eruption of the virus was slowing inside him as well as outside on the streets of Boston.

Sid took a long shower in the bathroom off the study. The steam gathered and filled the bathroom. He was under the shower for a good long time, sloughing off the disease. Afterwards, the water beaded and dripped down the tiles and the glass front of the shower. Sid dried himself. He looked out the window of the bathroom on the alleyway. The alleyway was deserted, but it was the light of a late morning. The trees at Sid's level were in fresh, mint green, filtering the light through their flickering leaves.

Angela had stripped the study clean of bedding. She was wiping surfaces with disinfectant. The windows were wide open, blowing a cool, stiff breeze through the study and into the hall. Sid padded down the hall with the towel wrapped around his waist. He stood in the doorway and felt the cool air. It reminded him of the country. Angela glared at him. He heard his name being called. Darrell wanted him to come down the stairs. He had some clothes he wanted Sid to put on, a turtleneck and some corduroy pants.

Sid sat in the living room on a leather ottoman while Paula and Angela, wearing masks, cut his hair and groomed his beard with an electric trimmer. He looked at himself in the mirror in the hall when they were done. He looked years younger. He had to look away. It was painful to see the transformation. It felt to him like losing an appendage, the version of himself as wandering lost in the wasteland. The apartment was an outcropping of some kind of illusion and the mirror was a portal into that new land he had not yet pierced. Sid was dubious, yet eager to start.

He applied himself to bitcoin and pound sterling. He wanted what Darrell had. Darrel explained early on that it had taken him two years of a graduate degree at Babson and several years of apprentice work at the trading desk of Morgan Stanley to really perfect his personal style. He warned Sid that it didn't come easy, none of it. Sid thought he could cut like a razor through the necessary information and get to the marrow of the bone, the skeleton of the corpse, so to speak, of the collapsing system that was the international currency exchange. They could chart its demise and feed from it, like the Beothuk had from schools of salmon spawning in the rivers of the northern forest. Here was the key that Jordan had sought, the language of money. It flowed like water, with streams that could only be seen on Darrell's computer screen in the graphs and charts, colored lines and bullet points that marked rapids and dams. Sid was a quick study, eager to cast his net, but Darrell was cautious. He had Sid practice on a currency trading simulator platform for a few weeks. Sid wanted to get into bitcoin. He thought it was a good bet against the deflationary pressures from the pandemic and coming economic collapse.

"Look at oil," said Sid. "That's gonna happen across the board."

Darrell was not so sure. They argued, with no resolution in sight, a simmering conflict brewing inside the Commonwealth Avenue apartment.

One night in the summer they watched a baseball game, the remnants of the season. Numbers of cases were holding steady for now in Massachusetts, but they were surging across the South. Darrell had it on the flat-screen above the kitchen area. He had some beers from Vermont. There were two glasses set on the marble counter filled with amber ale. Angela and Paula sat on the ottoman and went through dresses on Angela's iPad. Angela sipped from a goblet of Chianti Classico, while Sid and Darrell watched the baseball game and drank beers. The Red Sox were up two over the Orioles. The stands were largely empty, fans seated apart from each other to keep the Covid-19 at bay.

"Things are coming back," said Darrell.

"This dress sucks, *Mami*," said Paula.

"When's the prom now?" asked Darrell, looking at Sid. Sid looked at the flat screen, intent on catching the action as it happened.

"August, *mi corazon*," said Angela.

"That's what I'm saying," said Darrell. "Things are coming back. Slowly, but surely. We'll have Paris again, Angela. You wait." He winked at Sid and lifted his glass and took a long swallow. Sid tried to smile, but felt the bile rising in his throat like a tide.

"You like this one, Paula," said Angela.

"No, I don't," said Paula.

They went for a walk together, Sid and Darrell going out ahead, Angela and Paula lagging behind, looking at the Nordstrom and L'Elite Bridal storefronts. Some of the stores had reopened for business, with extended hours to accommodate requirements for customer spacing. There was a crowd of people out, all with the same idea in mind, of losing themselves in the hall of mirrors that was the consumer space. Sid and Darrell entered the Common as if fleeing from the domain of the women, and walked around and over the foot-bridges, a cruel absurdity for the two brothers that had once roamed the foothills and ancient trails of the Penacook and Kearsarge in the shadows of their warriors, thought Sid. Water flowed as the last of the day ebbed in the sky.

"I love this city," said Darrell. "I feel like I belong here. This is mine. I have a right to this. I own it," he said. "It's coming back. Boston strong."

"Good for you, Darrell," said Sid. For him, Boston was the repository of bitterness, the cloud of pestilence that had taken Patrick's life. It was the same historical process that had put him behind bars. They had all taken a wrong turn with lives that continued to veer out of control.

"The thing you don't get is nobody is going to let you play with their money based on your hunches. You need to have data to back it up. It's incremental, Sid. You need to take your time. You can't go with these ideas you come up with based on God knows what."

"I can see it. I can feel it. I want to play big on bitcoin. Let me have a chance."

"What if you're wrong? You're gonna be wrong."

"Were our ancestors wrong? Maybe they were. It doesn't matter. You stick with your instincts."

"Look, Sid. Get over it. Steve called himself a Beothuk. Whatever. He was more Irish than Beothuk. What is that, tap dancing? Be satisfied with the small steps. Data based. Then one day this can be yours, too." Darrell waved his hands in front of him as if ushering in the thinning crowd of pedestrians to join them.

"You don't understand, Darrell. I lived with more than twenty guys on a pod for nineteen years."

"I know you did. I'm sorry for that. That was fucked up. And you were innocent."

"No, I wasn't. I was guilty as charged."

"You're no more guilty than the average dude, Sid."

"We're all guilty. That's what makes me want to puke sometimes, Darrell. I have to keep moving."

"There's no amount of bitcoin that's going to help that," said Darrell.

"I know," answered Sid.

"We're killing this fucking planet. I wonder if there's going to be anything left for Paula. She's already said she doesn't want to have children. How messed up is that?" said Darrell.

"Steve had his art," said Sid. "Do you remember the wolf pack, Darrell?" asked Sid.

"Yeah. That was beautiful. But he was so messed up, man. The way he used to beat you. Don't even talk about his art. He had no willingness to save anybody but himself."

"Don't remind me. He's still alive, you know. I saw him."

"No, he's not. He's dead. He's buried in Lyndonville with Jan," said Darrell.

“I don't believe you. Then who was that in the house in Loonberg?” asked Sid.

“Some other guy. It wasn’t Steve,” said Darrell.

“I don’t believe you.”

“I’ll take you up to the graves, man.”

“Jan and Steve? Together?”

“Yeah. He wanted to be buried with her. Small town sweethearts. Even though she left him. In the end he left Yolanda.”

“What a dick,” said Sid.

“Agreed,” said Darrell.

“What about Yolanda?” asked Sid.

“I still get birthday cards from her. She’s in Florida. Outside of Tampa. Some retirement community. She’s remarried to a Marine. Vietnam vet like Steve,” said Darrell.

“Take me up there. I won’t believe it until I see the graves with my own eyes,” said Sid.

VII. Facts in the Ground

They drove up one day at the end of June. The highway was relatively free of traffic, just a few people with cars headed up to the mountains and lakes for an early weekend. You had to quarantine for two weeks to stay anywhere in New Hampshire. But restaurants were open. They stopped at Bow Junction for brunch. Sid got out of the car and felt the sun at his back. The parking lot was busy, colors flashing in the mid-morning light. He had a brief moment of deja vu, feeling like he could read the minds of the people in the cars, a cold wind whistling in his ears. But it went through him quickly, just an echo of the old sickness still ruminating in his bones. The sun on the back of his head and neck quickly drove away any vertigo. He shut his eyes and concentrated for a minute on the ease of his breathing. The restaurant was up some wooden steps lined with geraniums in pots. It was a new place, Texas style roadhouse, up the road before you got to Dunbarton. Paula had found it on Yelp. Angela and Paula waited at the door, reading the menu.

They removed their masks and ate baby back ribs, corn on the cob, and scrambled eggs with tortillas. They had apple pie and watermelon for dessert and finished with large coffees to go. They drank the coffee in Darrell's Infiniti. Angela took over the driving. She prided herself on her ability to evade police ambushes. She claimed she had a sixth sense. Darrell wanted to play some Latin music that Angela liked, but Paula insisted on silence. Sid sat in the back seat with Paula, enjoying the silence. Paula was doing an online course on anatomy. She had her earbuds in. Sid thought about the stages of life, the way they tumbled out of childhood and through adulthood like an avalanche, a burst of physical force and then a brief interlude of silence before it all melted away like the snow on the mountain tops.

They drove up 89 and then 91 into Vermont, the Northeast Kingdom, where Steve and Jan had grown up north of St. Johnsbury. They had gotten out of Lyndonville together when Steve had joined the Navy. He served his enlistment in Cam Ranh Bay and then worked for two more years as a diesel mechanic at the Portsmouth Shipyards. Then he'd gotten a discharge and disability pension due to health issues. Sid had been born about that time. Steve had bought the ramshackle, broken down property in Loonberg with savings, knocked it down and built it fresh. Sid had no memories of those years besides him and Darrell running through the snow on the driveway and climbing on piles of sodden chipboard and waste wood. The only picture he had of Jan in his mind was through the door in the bathroom, the only bathroom in the house, from a childhood afternoon as she did her hair, naked, her breasts showing, pendulous.

"Why did she leave?" asked Paula. She'd been listening the whole time, apparently, even with the earbuds.

"She was manic-depressive. She had moods. Steve drove her crazy. We don't really know," said Darrell.

"Very sad," said Angela, looking in the rear view mirror.

"Yolanda tried with Steve. But he was a hard guy to please," said Darrell. He reached for the radio button. This time Paula did not object. They listened to Eddie Palmieri and Mongo Santamaria on Sirius FM. Then they stopped at the Cumberland Farms outside St. Johnsbury.

Going up Route 5 looked familiar to Sid. He remembered driving this road with Steve and Jan when both he and Darrell were very young. They went up the hill past St. Elizabeth's church and parked in the lot across the road from the cemetery. Darrell knew where he was going. They walked towards the back of the cemetery along the path and the neat rows of headstones. Sid looked at the names: Roberge, Winkle, Cavanaugh, Nagle, Morency.

Darrell stopped, and they caught up to him.

Stephen C. Green-Smith

February, 1954 - July, 2014

Janice Marie Gibson

April, 1952 - March, 2005

"God Will Provide"

Two newish headstones, and the grass was mowed neatly. The sky was pale blue, and the wind was blowing high clouds past at the zenith. A flag at the entrance stood straight out momentarily and fell back again. Sid walked away.

"Look, there's some more Gibsons here," said Darrell. "We've got more cousins than we knew we had," said Darrell. "It was Jan's family that paid for the plots and the graves and tombstones."

Sid walked to the back of the cemetery, to the oval track that wound around it. Beyond the track was a hedge of pine trees and more woods behind it. He kicked at the gravel. There was some finality in seeing the gravestones of his mother and father, but like all things to do with Steve and Jan, there was something unknowable and slippery behind the apparent moment. Unknowable, slippery, but somehow familiar, as if he'd known and seen all of this before. He was disappointed that he didn't feel something new. It was just a fact that they had died and he'd never said goodbye, never held them, never really known them. Just ordinary sadness that did nothing for him. Or if it did, it just deepened his new found disgust at his former mental turmoil. Each new fact inevitably brought countless questions in its wake. Every question had an answer, but every answer led to more questions, exponential questions. The track led around on itself eventually, but you would recognize only the vaguest of signposts. You had learned nothing and only increased your levels of anxiety if you thought about it any more.

Sid turned around. Darrell, Angela, and Paula were each in a different part of the cemetery, wandering, staring at headstones, reading inscriptions. Sid was ready to leave, impatient with their efforts to memorialize in their separate ways. Sid wanted to listen to more music, keep driving somewhere else. He wanted to be with them, but they were straining to be apart from each other. People were frustrating to Sid, frustrating as they always were. Yet he could not be alone for long without drowning in mixed signals from afar and melting away from sequential reality.

Paula looked up. She and Angela were talking to each other. Sid approached Darrell.

"Seen enough?" asked Darrell.

"It's just sad," said Sid.

"Hey, it's normal to feel sad. They were our parents."

"So much nothing."

"I know what you mean. People have no idea, Sid. To end up dead. Maybe there's something afterwards. Who knows? If there is, maybe Steve wanting to be with Jan here in the end makes sense. He was a gambler, wasn't he?"

"Have to be. Always find a way to get back in the game."

"Exactly."

They walked back to the road. Darrell put his arm around Sid's broad shoulders as they wound along the track around the cemetery. Time slowed to the pace of their steps. Steve had been an artist, and Sid and Darrell had been a part of their father's art, and now there was another piece to it, this day that made it more beautiful, if not more meaningful. Maybe life was really a big work of art, a living sculpture that someday in vast aeons to come would make sense.

There was another place Sid wanted to go. He wanted to see the high school. He wanted them to drive to the Ferncroft Regional High School field. They sat in the car for a few minutes. Darrell was in the driver's seat. Angela prayed to herself, mumbling the words in Spanish. Sid asked Paula for a favor.

"Paula, find the number for the Pacha Mama in Concord."

Paula looked at him quizzically, and did something on her phone. She showed him the phone with the information displayed on the screen.

"Dial it for me, please."

Paula nodded. This was getting interesting, she seemed to suggest with her eyes. She took out the earbuds and handed Sid the phone as it rang. Sid stepped out of the car.

"Hello, can I speak with Ruth?"

"Just a second," said the woman who answered.

"Hello?"

"Ruth? It's Sid."

"Sid?"

"Yeah. It's me. I know, it's been awhile."

"Where are you?"

Sid felt that she was trying not to sound disturbed that he would dare call after all the time gone.

"I'm in Vermont. But I'm coming down to Loonberg. We're going to visit the high school. I'm with my brother, Darrell. I thought of you."

"It was Leesha's birthday last week. She's six now. You know, she always talks about you. She says, 'Sid likes macaroni and cheese, why can't Sid come eat dinner with us?' You know what I told her?"

"No. What did you tell her?"

"I said Sid is looking for his buried treasure. When he finds it he'll come see us. She misses you."

"I miss her, too. I need to see you, Ruth. Can you come up here?"

"You found your brother. That's something, Sid. Well, I'm getting off work now. I could pick Leesha up and meet you. We could go out to dinner, now that I'm getting paid again. Got my stimulus check, Sid. Did you get yours?"

"I've got some money. I've been working for my brother."

"Oh."

"Meet me at the high school, Ruth."

"Loonberg?"

"No, it's Ferncroft, remember?"

"Oh, yeah. The Fighting Woodcocks. I'll be there, Sid. Don't let me down this time."

"I won't. I promise."

They drove the hour or so back across the Whites, down the Kancamagus Highway and onto the rutted back road that wound down to Loonberg. The high school was at the end of the road between the two towns. Ferncroft had been in the old days a larger town, a farming town, and so the high school was named for it, but there had always been more Loonberg children in Sid and Darrell's day.

There were tall nettles growing under the bleachers. Ruth's car was parked against the fence, and she was running on the grass after Leesha. They had masks on their faces. Sid got out of the Infiniti and hopped the five foot fence instead of walking all the way to the gate. He jogged across the grass and noticed how dry and brittle it was. It hadn't rained in a couple of weeks. Some barn swallows swooped low, and clouds massed in the north. Leesha didn't break stride but ran around in a wide circle and headed for Sid. Sid fell to his knees at the 50 yard line. Ruth yelled. Leesha stopped running. Her eyes smiled at Sid. Ruth approached and picked Leesha up in her arms. It was quite a lift. Leesha was getting heavy.

"You're gettin big!" Sid laughed.

"Who are those people, Sid?"

"Yeah, that's Darrell, my brother, and his wife and his daughter."

"What are their names?"

"Oh, that would be Angela, his wife, and Paula, his daughter."

Sid waved at the three of them, Darrell, Paula, and Angela, leaning against the fence in the end zone and watching. It started to rain, a few thick, warm drops of water before the coming storm. They heard thunder. Ruth sat down with Leesha across from Sid.

"So this is it, huh. You played here?"

"This is where it happened, yup," said Sid, sitting straight. "I was just a kid, but it was like I was the big man in town for a couple of years. I could do no wrong."

"Until you did."

"Until I did. That's right."

Ruth sighed and shifted her weight. She played with Leesha's hair.

"I got sick, Ruth. I had the Chinese flu."

"Don't call it that."

"Okay. But I'm better now."

"Why do men always say they're better now? You don't know that," said Ruth.

"I am. I'm better now."

"Your words don't mean shit."

The rain pelted down as the clouds opened. He could see the small figures of Darrell, Paula, and Angela as they retreated back to the car. Sid felt like he was shouting to be heard over the blanketing noise of the rain.

“I promise you, Ruth. I know what I am and what I have been. We’re opening up, Ruth. It can be our time if we let it.”

“Are you going back with them? Looks like they’re leaving,” shouted Ruth.

“No, I’m done with all that crap,” said Sid, scooting closer. “I’m not interested. That’s not what’s up for me.”

“But they’re your family, Sid.”

“You're my family. You and Leesha.”

“You want to come back with us?”

“Yeah, Ruth. That’s what I want.”

“Ever since the first day I saw you on the park bench. You remember that?”

“Yeah.”

“What park was it?”

“White’s Park.”

"That's right. I said that's the guy for me. He can help me move the treadmill that's blocking up my life. You got my life going again."

"That's great, Ruth. You make me feel whole again. Like the hole in my heart is healed up."

A flash of lightning was followed almost instantly by a loud clap of thunder. They stood up. Ruth started jogging awkwardly with Leesha by the hand. Sid ran out in front of their path, knelt, and let Leesha climb up on his back. He sprinted for the gate in the end zone. His knees drove as he clasped Leesha's legs and she clung to his neck. His boots flew off. He was running like the old days, like time itself in the expanding sky, his feet clawing in the grass. He reached the end zone just as another flash of lightning lit up. It was almost on top of them.

He opened the passenger door on Ruth's car. Leesha dropped off of him and tumbled into the car. Ruth came through the gate. She flung open the driver-side door and threw his boots inside.

VIII. The Winter Leaves

A layer of frozen slush covered the road. The oak trees still had their leaves, blowing in the wind like ghastly ornaments in the November afternoon. The winter wind would strip them relentlessly of any vestige of their summer, thought Sid. Cars slowed as they took the turn on Pembroke Road. Sid was walking back to the apartment complex from the transfer station at the bottom of the hill before the entrance ramp to the highway. His days were spent sorting through the plastic and cardboard in the containers, finding any tainted pieces with food waste, piling them in the forklift to be driven over to the hopper, and carrying tires where they lay next to the brush, piling them for the truck from Casella, and helping the drivers with loading the tires into the truck.

In the spring they were supposed to take on another employee, the transfer station chief, James Bucco, had promised. In the interview, Bucco had warned Sid that the Chinese were getting pickier about what they took. The recycling business was going to depend more on manual sorting of trash to stay ahead of the lean times. The walk up the hill strained at his lungs. Sid's shoulders leaned forward, carrying the weight of the planet, his boots meeting the wet mix of road salt, dirt and undercarriage grease. The wind stung his bearded face around the exposed nose and ears. His hands were jammed in the pockets of his canvas coat, the fingers of the left hand tightly gripped around his pay stub, as he lifted his gaze into the steel blue of the eastern sky. In the fading twilight of rush hour, sedans and pickup trucks moved up and down Pembroke Road, taking little notice of the solitary pedestrian.

He'd been banished from life, relegated to incarceration and stripped of everything except his name, the name that he'd been born with and hung around his neck like some appendage of a past and a future eternally distant from his grasp. As he climbed the hill unafraid of the wind, Sid thought that the only meaning he'd gained out in the world again, reborn to the travails and pursuits of his country of the lost, had been just that sense of himself as adequate to the moment. It was, he thought, picking up his feet and trodding with the weighty step of a man half innocent but counted as guilty, a blessing and an honor to meet the trouble coming his way.

www.ingramcontent.com/pod-product-compliance
Lightning Source LLC
LaVergne TN
LVHW010614100826
845148LV00014B/2958
* 9 7 8 0 9 8 1 5 1 6 6 7 7 *